A bullet shattered the window.

Erica turned, trapped between train cars, with Nick battling a gunman on one side and the locked door on the other.

She couldn't believe it. The boy she'd loved and lost was back. And he was trying to save her son. The son Nick clearly knew nothing about.

"Erica!" he shouted. "Get ready to catch!"

She leaned around the corner just in time to catch the gun that skittered toward her.

"Get to the rear engine," Nick shouted. "I'll catch up with you."

She shot out the window to unlock the door. Then she froze. The engine car was empty. The phone was down, as was the radio. The security cameras were still on, though, and she saw a small, unmistakable form curled on a chair in the sights of two gunmen. Her breath caught in her throat.

Nick crashed through the door. "I took care of him. He—" He stopped when he met her eyes. "What's wrong?"

Her gaze turned to the monitor.

"They have my son."

Our son.

Maggie K. Black is an award-winning journalist and romantic suspense author with an insatiable love of traveling the world. She has lived in the American South, Europe and the Middle East. She now makes her home in Canada with her history-teacher husband, their two beautiful girls and a small but mighty dog. Maggie enjoys connecting with her readers at maggiekblack.com.

Books by Maggie K. Black

Love Inspired Suspense

True North Heroes

Undercover Holiday Fiancée
The Littlest Target
Rescuing His Secret Child

Amish Witness Protection

Amish Hideout

True North Bodyguards

Kidnapped at Christmas
Rescue at Cedar Lake
Protective Measures

Military K-9 Unit

Standing Fast

Visit the Author Profile page at Harlequin.com for more titles.

RESCUING HIS SECRET CHILD

MAGGIE K. BLACK

HARLEQUIN® LOVE INSPIRED® SUSPENSE

Recycling programs for this product may not exist in your area.

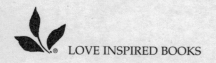

LOVE INSPIRED BOOKS

ISBN-13: 978-1-335-67888-1

Rescuing His Secret Child

www.Harlequin.com

Printed in U.S.A.

When I was a child, I spake as a child, I understood as a child, I thought as a child: but when I became a man, I put away childish things. For now we see through a glass, darkly; but then face to face: now I know in part; but then shall I know even as also I am known.
—1 Corinthians 13:11-12

With thanks to my wonderful agent, Melissa Jeglinski,
and talented editor, Emily Rodmell.
You both make me a stronger writer and enable me
to do things I never thought possible.

This book is because of "Zander."
Thank you for the stories.

ONE

Corporal Nick Henry dozed upright in an uncomfortable metal seat as the darkened train rumbled north through the rugged and inhospitable Ontario wilderness. A furtive hand brushed the sleeve of his green Canadian Army fatigues. A pickpocket was reaching for his service weapon! His eyes snapped open as he grabbed the offending hand by the wrist.

A small voice gasped. Nick turned. The hand belonged to a boy, probably no older than four or five, with wide green eyes and a messy mop of the kind of dark red hair that a woman Nick had once loved had told him to call "auburn." The boy wriggled. Nick let go. A dozen questions shot rapid-fire through the soldier's brain before he finally chose one. "Were you trying to take my gun?"

The boy scrunched up his nose as if Nick had

asked him something difficult. Nick shifted his weapon away and gave the child a second to come up with an answer as he glanced at his phone. It was quarter after eleven and they'd already entered the cell tower dead zone. Spring winds shrieked outside. Rain buffeted fierce and wild against the windowpanes. Around them, scattered passengers stretched out and slept the best they could in the half-empty economy car.

Where had this kid come from? Nick hadn't seen any children when he'd boarded. He imagined most families with kids that young wouldn't take an overnight train north but would pick a more reasonable time when they could look out at the towering and jagged rocks, thick trees and dazzling lakes that still filled the parts of northern Ontario untouched by roads and buildings. Not to mention when the dining car was still open. "Where are your parents?"

The boy dodged the question with an ease that reminded Nick of his younger self by returning his question with one of his own. "Are you really a soldier? A real one?"

A real one? Nick felt a smile curl at his lips. It was an interesting question. One that Nick had asked himself more times then he'd liked to admit as an impetuous teenager in his early days of boot camp when he'd been trying to stop sabotaging himself, get over his own worse impulses and step up to be the kind of man he'd wanted to be. But it was definitely not an answer to the boy's question. Then again, at least the kid was talking.

"Yup, I am one hundred percent a real soldier," Nick continued, seeing as the boy seemed to be waiting for more of an answer. He stood as his eyes scanned for anyone missing a child. "I'm Corporal Nick Henry, of the Canadian Armed Forces, stationed out of Petawawa in northern Ontario. I'm currently heading even farther north to teach firearms safety, self-defense and wilderness survival to a new group of Canadian Ranger reservist recruits."

He glanced at the kid and realized he'd just given him the pat answer he'd give anyone who asked. Nick twisted his lips and tried to think of how to say it again in words a child would understand. "I've been a soldier for six years, almost. My title is corporal. That means I'm in command of other soldiers, but also that I'm kind of new at it. I train people in Canada to survive disasters and protect each other. You can call me Nick." He stretched out his hand. "What should I call you?"

"Zander." Earnest eyes looked up at him. "With a *Z*. My mommy calls me her little soldier. 'Cause my grandpa and great-grandpa used to be in the army, and I remind her of them."

Pride tinged the boy's voice and it tugged at something inside Nick.

"Nice to meet you, Zander." They shook hands. "Now, how about we go find your family?"

Zander shook his tousled curls and Nick was almost jealous for when he'd been able to let his hair grow that long and shaggy. "I need to borrow your gun."

Nick chuckled, "Why do you need my gun?"

"I need to protect my mommy." Zander's voice dropped to a whisper.

The smile faded instantly from Nick's face and he could tell it had taken the color with it. "Why?"

The boy's chin rose defiantly. "I saw bad men. They have guns."

Bad men with guns. The words echoed in Nick's head, merging with prayers for wisdom. A year before he'd been born, Nick's sister had been killed by a "bad man" when she was a child. But his three older brothers still remembered, each in their own way, the day she'd died fighting off her would-be abductor. He'd grown up in a deeply loving family that had swirled with a grief he hadn't understood and then had acted out in foolish and immature ways he was still ashamed of. He swallowed hard and forced the memory into the recesses of his mind, where things he didn't want to think about went to fade.

He searched the child's face for even a flicker of insincerity and found none. It was possible, if not probable, that either the boy's imagination was playing tricks on him or that he'd been asleep and had a nightmare. "Where are the bad men? Are they on the train?"

Zander craned his neck to look up at him. The slight quiver to his chin told Nick that as far as the boy was concerned the danger was real. A wave of empathy pushed Nick's legs to bend until he was crouching at the boy's eye level. The youngest of four brothers, all now over six feet, he remembered all too well what it was like to feel small. Now, here, someone little was looking up to him for help. He prayed he wouldn't let him down.

"They're in the dining car," Zander said. "It's in between the part of the train with the big fancy cabins with bed seats and here. That's where Mommy was supposed to be."

That meant the boy had walked through two mostly empty economy cars looking for help. Also, Nick had been sure the dining car was closed.

"How many men?" Nick asked. The boy shrugged. Either he didn't know or couldn't remember. "Did they see you?"

"No, I was hiding under the tables playing and waiting for Mommy." He mimed clutching an invisible weapon to his side. "They were hiding the guns under the table like this."

Nick glanced up at the red emergency button, knowing that all it would take was a swift slap to get a siren to sound and the train's conductor to rush in. The engineers might even initiate an emergency stop. If the boy was wrong, it would cause a whole lot of chaos. But if the boy was right... He closed his eyes. *Lord, what do I do?*

Then a small hand clutched his and squeezed. "Please, Soldier Nick, we've got to help my mommy."

"Don't worry, we'll find her." Nick squeezed back. Then he straightened and pulled his rucksack over his shoulder. They started through the train. "What about your father?"

"He's a good-for-nothing hothead who's probably in prison," Zander said almost cheerfully and Nick suspected he'd overheard the words more than once but wasn't sure what they meant. "I was supposed to stay in the fancy seats with my uncle and his friend. But my uncle fell asleep and his friend went for a walk and I was bored, so I went to find Mommy."

"And you didn't see any conductors or train attendants?"

Another head shake. Not that train conductors were armed, even though one of the roles they served was as security.

They reached the end of the economy-class car and Nick slid the door open. Stepping into the shaking, rattling space between the two train cars, they crossed over the joint that held one car to the next. Then they walked through the next two economy cars. Nick scanned his fellow passengers as they went, hoping to spot a fellow service member or a cop like his brothers Trent and Jacob, or a paramedic like his brother Max—anyone he could count on in a crisis. He came up short, with the exception of an elderly gentleman he suspected had once served, and a sleeping brute with the build that suggested he might've worked as a bodyguard.

He didn't spot any guards or train staff, either. That worried him.

They reached the end of the economy cars and entered the no-man's-land between it and the dining car.

"The bad men are in there." Zander pointed at the door. "Mommy s'posed to be there, too, but she wasn't. Can I have your gun now? Mommy won't let me shoot a gun yet. But I've seen her shoot flying disks right out of the sky. She punches, too." His tiny fists mimed punching a bag. "She's really good at it."

Go, Zander's mom! Nick could guess where the kid got his gumption. If it turned out the boy was right, and there was danger on the train, maybe Zander's mother wouldn't be the worst person to be in it with.

"No, but you can borrow my bulletproof vest and helmet, if you like. But you have to promise to stay exactly where I tell you to stay and not move."

The boy nodded. Nick took his bulletproof vest and helmet out of his rucksack and carefully helped Zander into them.

"Thank you," Zander whispered. "Now I really do look like a little soldier."

"You're welcome." He'd done it mostly to soothe the boy's fears. And yet, as he looked into Zander's serious face. Nick felt some unfamiliar emotion tighten in his own throat, like a longing for something he'd never had.

Nick glanced through the small, thick glass window into the dining car. So much for it being closed. A tall, thin man in a suit, who looked to be in his late forties, sat reading a newspaper by the far door. In the opposite corner, a young couple in hoodies sat staring at the table. In the middle of the car, three tattooed and bearded men in heavy plaid jackets drummed their fingers on the table with the telltale twitches of people missing a nicotine fix.

Yeah, those last three practically had "bad men" written across their faces. If his Vice detective brother Trent had been there, he'd have probably pegged their gang affiliation at a hundred paces. Not that it meant they were armed or up to no good at this very moment.

The door opened at the far end of the dining car. A woman walked through, her head bowed, pushing a narrow refreshment cart. Her hair was auburn and tied back in a braid, a few loose waves falling around her downturned face. Her crisp blue train attendant's uniform, with its sharp blazer and knee-length skirt, only seemed to accentuate her lithe, strong form.

"That's my mommy!" Zander said.

Well, then, Zander's mom was a knockout as well as, apparently, a force to be reckoned with. Although the kid could've explained earlier that his mother worked for the train company. He'd get Zander to stay behind, with his helmet and vest to play with, signal her and get her into the next car. Then he'd explain the situation and, if there really was a problem, they could alert the conductor.

She looked up.

He stepped back involuntarily, as huge dark eyes fringed with long, beautiful lashes scanned the window where he stood. And suddenly a hundred conflicting memories struck him at once, overwhelming his senses like a flurry of fists hitting his core.

He remembered meeting those same dark eyes across grade school, junior high and high school classrooms.

He remembered running through the trees between his farm and the farm next door, way too late at night, in the hope that the same face would appear at the window.

He remembered what it had been like to finally let his guard down at nineteen, to tell her how his sister Faith's murder had left him with a self-destructive pain that sometimes made him want to blow up everything good in his life and push away the people he cared the most about.

He'd told her she was beautiful and the best person he'd ever met. He'd pulled her into his arms. Then he'd failed to stand up like a man and face her disappointment when Tommy, her hotheaded older brother, had found them, yanked them apart and told Erica she deserved far better than an irresponsible loser who got into stupid fights, barely scraped through high school and had no future ahead of him.

He cringed as the memory of what had happened next filled his mind. He'd stormed off, got drunk, raced to see her and apologize— even propose, as if a sloppy, rushed proposal was what a woman like her deserved—then lost control of his brother's car and wrapped it around a tree. How he'd paced the jail cell he'd been tossed into on a drunk driving charge while waiting for his folks to come bail him out. How he'd promised God he was done being that guy. That he'd make something of his life, join the army and become the man she'd needed him to be.

All of it, every glorious and sorry moment, seemed to hit him in a glance.

Zander's mother was Erica Knight.

She was the only girl he'd ever cared about. The one he'd lost. The one he'd known he'd never deserved.

As he watched, the tall, thin man in the suit rose from his seat and held a gun to Erica's side.

Erica's breath caught in her throat as she felt the barrel of the gun press deep into her ribs. Just a few seconds earlier her biggest concerns had been the fact that Bob Bass, the front engineer, had a tendency to show up hungover and that the rainstorm was so heavy the train would have to take a slower route to Moosonee in case the bridge over the Moose River flooded. That and the fact the normally empty first-class car now had seven passengers spread over three of the four sleeper cabins. Nine passengers if you counted the fact her brother, Tommy, had snagged seats for him and Zander in one of the sleeper cabins thanks to a rather sleazy friend of his from high school—Clark Lemain, who had somehow rehabilitated his image enough to convince their community to elect him as a provincial politician. Clark relentlessly asked her out for coffee whenever he rode first-class, seeming to think the fact she had to serve him drinks and snacks meant she wanted to spend time with him, and also tended to make presumptuous comments about Zander needing a father. She didn't exactly like the idea of Clark getting closer to her son.

But now the pressure of metal against her ribs had blocked out all thoughts but whether anyone else in the train was also in danger and how to get herself and everyone out of whatever this was alive.

Including her son.

She breathed a prayer of thanksgiving that Zander was tucked safely with her brother and Clark. The first-class car had both a large common lounge area and four cabins with doors that closed and locked, with seats that converted into beds. Her dislike of the showy politician who'd booked it notwithstanding, Zander was much safer there than with the regular passengers.

"Stay calm." The voice in her ear was low

and menacing, with the hint of a fake and practiced smile. The man shifted his body so that the gun was slightly behind her and hidden by his jacket. Nobody else in the dining car seemed to have noticed. "Look straight ahead. Do exactly what I say, and nobody needs to get hurt."

His name was Mr. G. Grand. Or at least that was what his ticket had said when she'd checked it not ten minutes earlier on her pass through the dining car on the way to get her food cart. He'd boarded in Toronto and was riding the train all eight hours to Moosonee. Zander's father used to say she had a photographic memory. It was more that she was good at paying attention to things and wasn't quick to forget what she'd seen, which was handy when it came to keeping track of who'd actually booked a first-class ticket and who was just trying to sneak in.

She took a deep breath and let it out slowly, praying as she did so. The man's movement had been so quick and smooth she hadn't even realized what was happening until the gun was pressed against her. None of the passengers in the dining car had looked up or even moved a muscle.

The young pair huddled to her left were Rowan and Julie Baker. Brother and sister, she thought and rather young for first class, and yet their tickets had checked out. His beard was scraggly, and her large glasses, pale hair and skin gave her a fragile quality. Neither, she imagined, would be much good in a crisis. The three burly, tattooed men to her right looked like they'd been in their fair share of fights. Though all had a twitchiness that didn't fill her with much confidence.

All five seemed oblivious to the man now standing behind her, whispering threats in her ear. If life had taught her anything, it was that most people were too caught up in their own stuff to even notice when anybody else needed them.

Lord, I could really use some help right now.

Her eyes scanned the empty window at the very end of the car. She thought she'd seen someone there a moment ago. A soldier. Tall, with short dark hair, broad shoulders and an oval face that somehow jarringly reminded her of the man she'd unrequitedly loved and then lost six years ago. Nick Henry. But Nick wasn't a soldier. He was reckless, immature and the last person who'd ever come to her rescue.

No, she was on her own. And the most important thing she could do now was to de-escalate the situation before anyone got hurt.

"What do you want?" she asked softly, keeping her voice calm and clear.

"You're going to walk with me to the baggage compartment," Mr. Grand whispered. "Nice and slow. No sudden movements. Then when we get there, you're going to unlock one of the cabinets, take out a case and hand it to me."

A simple theft, then. The northern Ontario town and port of Moosonee, in the southern tip of James Bay, was the main access port to the Arctic and completely inaccessible by road. It was train, plane or nothing, which meant all sorts of packages and pieces of equipment were shipped by rail.

The train company's rules about robbery were clear. Staff was supposed to cooperate, to give the thief whatever was wanted and to remember that everything was heavily insured. There were sixty-seven passengers on the train right now and seven other train employees. No theft was worth risking all those lives. And yet the idea of letting some criminal just rob someone galled something inside Erica. She wanted to trip the closest security alarm. She wanted to pick up the entire serving cart, hurl it at his head and knock the gun from his grasp. But no. She'd put the lives of everyone on the train ahead of her own fighting instinct and do what needed to be done.

"I'll take it and get off at Coral Rapids," he went on. "You will not alert anyone until the train has left the station for at least an hour."

Or what exactly? She nodded again so he'd think she was cooperating. But her mind spun, accessing the situation like she was back in math class and someone had just presented her with a logistics problem.

Coral Rapids was a flag stop, meaning that someone had to actually have requested it. That also meant they were unlikely to pick up or drop off any other passengers there, especially at this time of night. After that, it was a three-hour nonstop run to Moosonee. Her eyes darted to the watch on her wrist. But Coral Rapids was twenty minutes away and it would only take a few moments to walk to the baggage car and unlock the cabinet.

And why grab a train attendant in the dining car in front of potential witnesses? The train was nine cars long. The baggage car was at the very back, second to last and right before the rear engine. The dining car was third from the front, after the front engine and first-class car. Why make her walk all the way through several economy cars to get to the back of the train? Why not grab another member of the train staff? Preferably someone already in the rear engine car.

She glanced at the security cameras. For that matter, how wasn't anyone seeing this? There were camera feeds in both the front and rear engines.

The gun pressed deeper. He leaned closer. "Do I have to tell you what will happen to your little boy if you don't cooperate?"

He knew about Zander!

Fear poured over her limbs as tears rushed to her eyes. Was that why he'd nabbed her? Because he knew she was traveling with her son? She gritted her teeth and refused to let the tears fall. "I'll cooperate."

"Okay, then, let's go. Slowly."

She maneuvered her way around the cart, feeling Mr. Grand close behind her. Zander's cheeky grin and bright green eyes filled her mind. In spite of his flaws, including a few youthful brushes with the law, mostly for brawling and causing a disturbance, Tommy was a devoted uncle. Her brother loved Zander and would keep him safe, despite the fact she occasionally had to rake Tommy over the coals for privately calling her son "the mistake."

True, falling into Nick's arms that night had never been part of her plan—let alone what she'd imagined was God's plan—for her life. She'd become pregnant at eighteen by an irresponsible young man who'd decided he'd rather disappear than step up.

Zander's birth had forced her to slow her Queen's University criminology degree to just a single course a semester as she'd juggled part-time work and single motherhood to rebuild her life in a whole new town.

According to Tommy, when he'd told Nick she was pregnant, Nick had denied the baby was his and told her brother to get lost. But still, if Zander's father had been the one who'd taught her to be herself, to trust her instincts, to climb, fight and even to shoot, Zander was the one who'd taught her she was far stronger and more resilient than she'd ever imagined.

She kept walking through the dining car, focusing on just taking one step after another.

Keep it together, Erica. You're not the cop or

criminologist you once hoped to be. You're just a train attendant with a job to do. Your son's life and the life of every passenger on this train depends on you.

The door slid open at the end of the car. But she barely had time to register the solider standing there, before a small boy in a heavy green vest and oversize military helmet darted out from behind the soldier and tried to run down the aisle toward her, even as the soldier shouted at him to stop.

"Mommy, no!" Zander called. "He's a bad man!"

Her heart stopped, barely registering that the other five dining-car passengers had turned. Zander tripped from the weight of his incongruous military gear, tumbling over himself as he landed on the floor in front of her. His tiny chin shook as tears filled his eyes. She reached for him. Mr. Grand's hand landed hard on her shoulder, pressing the gun deeper into her ribs, holding her in place.

"Please!" Her voice rose to a cry. "I need to help my son!"

Then, even before she could blink, a second figure shot through the door. It was a soldier in the green military fatigues of the Canadian

Armed Forces. His dark head bent low as he threw himself toward her little boy, sweeping him into his arms and cradling him protectively to his chest. The soldier dropped to one knee.

A prayer of thanksgiving exploded through her chest. Then her son's protector looked up, his piercing, deep green eyes rising to meet hers.

It was Nick Henry.

It was Zander's father.

He kept his right arm wrapped around Zander, pulled his service weapon with his left and aimed it at Mr. Grand.

"Sir," Nick said, "I don't want to cause a scene, but I have to ask you to please raise your hands and step away from the lady."

Oh, Nick, I don't know how or why you're here but...

The trio of burly men in plaid to her right rose sharply. The young couple to her left rose, too. One flick of Mr. Grand's hand and all five pulled out guns and aimed them at the man she'd once loved and the son he'd chosen to abandon.

They were surrounded.

TWO

As she watched, the three burly and tattooed men moved swiftly to lock both dining-car doors and keep anyone from entering or exiting. Nick tightened his grip on Zander, pulling him deeper into his chest. Suddenly it hit her—Nick must have given up his protective gear to shield Zander.

A lump filled Erica's throat. Nick was willing to take a bullet for the boy he'd apparently told her brother couldn't possibly be his. Tommy had told him about Zander, right? Her brother was overprotective and could be a bit of a hothead, but he wouldn't have lied to her about that. A thousand questions flooded her mind. But any answers would have to wait.

She watched as Nick's shoulders straightened. Gone was the cute, lanky farm boy with shaggy dark hair that flopped over his eyes, replaced instead by a man with a sharp military haircut and broad muscular chest that tapered to long, strong legs, now crouched to spring.

But somehow, as he looked up at her, the half smile that brushed his generous lips was exactly the same as it'd always been.

"Hey, Erica," he said. His eyes lingered on her face but his gun was pointed directly and unwaveringly at the man behind her. "This is quite the boy you have here. He tells me he's your son."

Her son. Not "theirs" in other words. She had no clue what to make of that. But Nick had always been both impetuous and reckless, and the last thing this situation needed was for him to suddenly discover that the five-year-old boy clutched to his chest was his son. There was no telling what Nick would do.

Or what Mr. Grand would do...

The thief's five-person crew still surrounded them with their guns at the ready, presumably waiting for Mr. Grand to tell them what to do. But the tall, thin man had fallen silent. She imagined that whatever he'd planned hadn't involved a standoff in the dining car with an armed soldier. But the longer they stalled, the more opportunity there was for someone in the rear engine, front engine or conductor's booth to see what was happening on the cameras and take action.

Erica nodded to Nick, finding no words up to the task of expressing anything she was thinking, and instead glanced down at her little boy.

"Hey, Little Soldier," she said softly. "You're having quite the adventure tonight, aren't you? Now, you stay still and quiet for Mommy, okay? Don't worry, everything's going to be okay."

Zander nodded. His eyes met hers from the small gap between the military helmet and Nick's strong arm. They were the same color as his father's.

"I told your son to stay behind me and out of the dining car," Nick said. "But it appears he's as headstrong as his mother."

And as impetuous and difficult as his father. What was Nick saying? That he'd had the ability to stop her son from being in danger and instead he'd let a five-year-old boy slip past him and run toward a gunman? Frustration burned in her gut. Nick's outside shell might've matured and grown. But it seemed inside Nick was the same irresponsible guy who'd drunkenly slammed his older brother's car into a tree.

"Stand up, soldier," Mr. Grand said. "Raise your hands and drop your weapon."

"I'm afraid I can't do that, sir," Nick said calmly, "because it would mean letting go of this young man here and I'm not about to put him in danger. So, how about we all put our weapons down, you let his mother go and we find a way to settle this without anyone getting hurt?"

There was something so incredibly gutsy about Nick's calm and self-control, she didn't know whether to be horrified or impressed. Her heart settled on a mixture of both.

The young woman named Julie was shaking. Clearly whatever was going on, the waif-thin blonde had never held a gun before and wasn't sure how to shoot it. Julie's brother, Rowan, wasn't doing much better although he was clutching the gun with two hands. They didn't really seem like an obvious fit for a gang of thieves. But the tattooed trio looked like they wouldn't hesitate to put a bullet through someone's head.

All this for a single case? Again, Erica's eyes flickered to the security cameras and then to the door behind Nick. But still nobody came. Something was very wrong. Nick's jaw set.

He'd always had an indestructible quality to him. Like no matter what life threw at him, it just all bounced off, leaving him unscarred. Until that one night he'd told her about his sister's murder and it was like he'd suddenly broken wide open… She blinked hard and forced the memory from her mind. No matter how strong Nick had seemed, he wasn't bulletproof. And neither was their son.

"How about this?" Nick asked. "I'll drop my weapon if you agree to remove the woman and child from the equation. You let them go into the first-class car, put a guard on the door if it makes you feel any better, and I'll put my gun down and we can talk."

So, Nick was going to go up against half a dozen armed criminals in exchange for her and Zander? He didn't know the first thing about this train, how to get a case from the cabinet or even what Mr. Grand wanted. The Nick she'd once known and loved had been strong, brave, gutsy and daring. But he didn't think, he didn't plan and now he was going to get himself killed. She felt the train begin to slow. Coral Rapids was drawing closer.

Nick's legs flinched like he was preparing to take action.

"Mr. Grand, you win!" Erica's hands shot up high over her head. "Your deal is with me, not him. Leave Nick out of this. He can't help you, but I can. The train is going to hit the next station in a few minutes. You're in a hurry to grab that case and get out of here, and I'm still willing to take you to the baggage car and get it for you. If you knew I had a son, then you probably know his uncle is now with a friend in the first-class car. Let me take him there, leave him with them, and then we'll walk back through the train together to the rear baggage compartment and get that case." Her eyes cut to Nick's face. She held his gaze in a vise grip.

"Nick, let Zander go. I know exactly what Mr. Grand wants and how to get it for him. I don't need your help."

Seconds ticked by. Nick's head shook. His eyes implored her to trust him and to let him handle it. She knew that look and she'd done that once. She wouldn't now.

"Fine," Mr. Grand grunted. He pointed to Julie, Rowan and a dark-haired thug with sunken cheeks. "You two and Lou come with me to drop off the boy with his uncle." He nodded to the tallest thug and the bearded brute in turn. "Orson, Fox, stay here, keep an eye on our soldier and make sure he doesn't get any bright ideas."

Oh, she imagined Nick had a ton of bright ideas. But she was also right, and she knew it. Mr. Grand stepped back. She knelt down and opened her arms for Zander. Nick let him go and the small boy slipped from his grasp and into her arms.

"I found a real soldier, Mommy," Zander's arms tightened around her. "A grown-up one. I got him to come help."

"You did a very good job." She lifted him and hugged him to her chest.

"Do you think he'll let me keep the helmet and vest?" Zander asked.

"I think he will for now."

"You can't let the bad guys win, Mommy," Zander whispered. "You're really brave and strong."

His simple, childlike faith in her sent guilt stabbing her heart. Zander believed in her. What example was she setting by surrendering? And yet was there any possible way to stop the gang of thieves without putting Zander's life at risk? No case was worth losing him over.

They walked through the dining car, with

her son in her arms, Mr. Grand leading the way
and the three others to her back.

There was one option—only one—and
they'd have to be quick. There was a security-
alarm button just above the doorway to the
first-class train car. She couldn't reach it. Not
without being seen. But Zander could. She bent
her head close to his and whispered, "Do you
think when we go under the door you can press
the red emergency button for me? Smack it really hard. I'll tell you when. You'll need to do
it really sneaky and super fast."

Zander nodded seriously. She hugged him
tightly.

It was a risk she hated taking. But she
couldn't reach it without alerting attention.
All it would take was a little jostle at the right
moment and she could hoist Zander up high
enough that he could do it. And that would
be that. The alarm would sound. Conductors
would come. Or at the very least, somebody
would finally look at the security cameras, alert
police and have them waiting for them when
they pulled into the station.

She'd use the distraction to sprint through the
lounge area, clutching Zander to her chest, dive
into the closest sleeper cabin, lock the door,

hide under the sleeper chair with her son and pray for rescue. Yes, it would be putting their lives at risk. And she'd be leaving Nick alone and in the line of fire. But what other option did she have? Leave Zander with her brother and his insufferable friend while being guarded by armed criminals?

She held her breath and held him high, prayers filling her heart. They crossed under the emergency alarm.

"Now." She jostled Zander against the wall. His tiny hand jutted up and smacked the button hard. She held her breath and waited for the alarm to sound.

Nothing happened.

So somebody had disabled the alarm, Nick thought as he watched Zander's nimble hand shoot up and press what he guessed was the emergency button. Either that or Zander hadn't struck it hard enough, which didn't seem likely. Thankfully, none of the criminals seemed to have noticed what the small boy had tried to do. Plus, the kid was impressively quick.

Erica had been the whole reason he'd joined the military to begin with. She'd always been so proud of her late father and grandfather for serving and believed in stepping up and serving one's country. And she called her son "Little Soldier." His heart didn't begin to know how to make heads or tails of any of that. Of anything, really. So for now he stood back and watched as Erica, Zander and their armed escort disappeared into the first-class car.

Nick kept his gun steady and aimed at the tall and bald thug, who Mr. Grand had called Orson, who now stood closest to the door. The bearded man, who apparently went by Fox, stood at the opposite end of the dining car with his gun. For now, Nick waited. Never a comfortable place to be.

It seemed Erica was every bit as gutsy as he remembered. Although she'd been incredibly wrong to step in like that and sideline him. He was a military corporal. He was trained in handling conflicts and this wouldn't have even been the first or second armed standoff he'd talked his way out of.

But apparently all Erica could see when she looked at him was the irresponsible young man he'd once been. No wonder she hadn't responded to his heartfelt letter.

And how had he not known that Erica Knight had a son?

He'd written to her about two months after the night his world had been blown apart—apologizing, pledging to be a better man, telling her about joining the military, begging her forgiveness. He'd walked the letter over personally in the hope of hand delivering it and asking her forgiveness in person. Her brother, Tommy, whom Nick had never got along with at the best of times, had met him at the end of the driveway, told him that Erica had moved to Kingston to go to Queen's University and never wanted to hear from Nick ever again.

Now he was surprised that Tommy hadn't chosen to twist the knife in even deeper by telling him that Erica had quickly moved on to a new man. Then again, judging by what Zander had said about his father, it sounded like Erica was better off without him.

As he stared at the empty space where Erica had been just moments ago, he felt an uncomfortable thought cross his mind. Zander was five. It had been almost six years since Nick had seen Erica. If it'd been any of his buddies standing in his boots, he'd have asked them how they could be sure Zander wasn't their son. But as soon as he felt the question of whether Zander was his begin to form, he pushed it away firmly. No. He may not know much in this world, but he knew Erica's character. Erica wouldn't have kept that from him. Not her. Yes, he'd been irresponsible. Yes, he'd hurt her badly. But she was sweet, honest and kind. The idea that she'd keep his own son from him was utterly unthinkable…

"Drop the gun," Fox snapped. "Kneel down and put your hands on your head. Or I'll put a bullet through your skull."

Nick pondered pointing out to Fox that he could do that, though probably not fast enough to keep Nick from putting a bullet through Orson first. But something told him Fox didn't much care. These two and Lou were hired guns, he guessed, nothing more, and just doing a little freelance thuggery for the suited man Erica had called Mr. Grand. Fewer thieves probably meant a bigger cut for whoever was left standing at the end. Stories from his brother Trent's undercover Vice days had taught him there was a certain criminal element that was willing to take on any job for a price.

How the younger pair had got involved was a bit more of a mystery, because unless Nick was very much mistaken, neither of those two had ever held a gun in their lives, let alone fired one. Then again, there was a first time for everything. If Mr. Grand was after a case in the baggage car, it seemed like he'd gone to a huge amount of trouble to steal it.

Nick glanced from the criminal behind him to the criminal in front of him. Could he shoot them both before either one of them managed to hit him with a bullet? Maybe. Maybe not. But he'd be selfish to risk his life in a shootout when Erica and her son needed him.

Slowly he set the gun down and knelt.

"So, fellas," he said, "I think I've got this thing all figured out. But maybe you can fill in some of the blanks for me. I gather that Mr. Grand is the big boss man and he brought the two of you, plus a third hired gun, in on the heist. He steals an important thing. You wave your guns around and walk away at the end with a big payday. All that I get. But what I don't understand is why he involved a couple of newbie kids. Or what could possibly be in the case that's worth enough cash to make your cut of it worth your while. Because I'm guessing hiring guys like you doesn't come cheap."

"Shut your mouth," Fox snarled, tossing in a couple of swear words for good measure. Okay, Nick took that as an affirmative that he was on the right track, not that he had any idea where that track was leading him yet. "If you try anything, we'll kill you and tell Mr. Grand that you tried to make a run for it."

He didn't doubt it. Nick's eyes rose to the ceiling. He listened to the rain beating against the outside of the metal tube they were traveling in, and prayed. He'd never been any good at being still and waiting. Even when he was supposed to be standing at attention he could feel his fingers fidgeting.

Kneeling there, with two guns pointed at opposite sides of his head was probably the most excruciating moment of his life. Then, when Erica stepped back into the dining car, flanked by Mr. Grand, his eyes fell on her face, and just like he had so many years ago, he found himself telling God that he'd do anything in his power to protect her.

"Nick..." She whispered his name like she wasn't quite sure he was really there. "Are you okay?"

He nodded. Her hand reached for him and instinctively he reached back into the empty air between them. He rose, his legs braced to drop to the floor at any moment if somebody gave him the command to stop. Nobody did. Instead he was vaguely aware as Mr. Grand nodded to Fox to unlock the far door.

Then Erica's fingers brushed against his and Nick was overwhelmed by the feeling of her hand sliding into his palm.

He pulled her to his side. "Is Zander okay?" he asked quickly.

Her eyes met his for the briefest moment and he watched the gold flecks dance against the sea of coffee brown. "Yeah. He's with Tommy and Clark in a sleeper cabin. Rowan, Julie and Lou are guarding them. He's scared but I think having your helmet and vest is helping. He's a pretty brave and strong kid."

"Seems it," he said. "I had no idea you had a child."

Her eyes widened. Her hand faltered in his and, for a moment, he thought her fingers were going to fall from his grasp. "Tommy told you!"

"No, he didn't." His head shook. "Why would your brother ever tell me something like that?"

To hurt him? To make him feel worse about losing the only woman he'd ever really cared about? At least this was the final nail in the coffin of any lingering question of whether Zander was his son. The Erica he'd known would've told

He found himself praying hard that Erica was right and Mr. Grand and his crew would quickly and quietly leave the train at Coral Rapids.

They reached the baggage car. The train jolted, and he felt Erica fall against his side. Her lips brushed his ear so quickly he barely caught her furtive whisper. "When I give the signal, run to the rear engine and alert the guards."

What? Without her? He scanned her face, but her gaze had dropped to her watch.

"Get the door," Mr. Grand commanded. Erica pulled her hand away from Nick's and punched a pass code into the keypad by the door. They stepped into the baggage car. Metal cages, shelves and footlockers lined the walls, filled with suitcases, sports equipment and packages of every conceivable shape and size. Even a very impressive motorcycle. Why go for a single case when someone could rob an entire train? No road access meant even the mail came by train.

Lord, what am I missing? Why steal one case? Why didn't the alarm go off? Where is the rest of the train staff? Why isn't someone noticing this on the security cameras? Please, help me get what's going on here and what I'm supposed to do about it.

They walked through the baggage car to a tall metal cabinet. "Open it."

Erica nodded and punched another code into the cabinet's keypad. The door swung open.

"That one!" Mr. Grand pointed to a briefcase that sat high on a shelf. "Get it down!"

Erica stood on her tiptoes and Nick was impressed at how well she kept her balance in high-heeled shoes. The large case was silver, with a double locking system, like the high-security cases he'd seen his detective brothers use for keeping evidence and weapons. It was the kind of case he'd have expected to see handcuffed to whoever had been assigned to transport it, not sitting alone in a baggage compartment. Chalk that up as another thing on the big list of things that made no sense.

The train slowed beneath them. Any moment now, they'd be in the station.

Erica set the case on the floor and Nick blinked as a name and logo came into view: North Jewels Diamond Mine.

He blinked again. Yeah, definitely not the kind of case he'd expect to see unaccompanied. Was this a jewel heist? North Jewels Diamond Mine was located in a very remote area of Canada's Arctic, accessible only by tiny prop planes flying out of airports like Moosonee. His brother Trent had helped in a huge undercover operation that had proved multiple high-level staff had been coordinating with unknown government officials to siphon diamonds from the mine's operations into organized crime. Last he'd heard, some arrests had been made and trial dates had been set, but witnesses weren't talking.

"Open it," Mr. Grand said. "Combination is two, eight, seven, one, pound."

Erica knelt and fiddled with the dial.

The case clicked open and Nick held his breath. No diamonds. Instead a shiny black laptop sat inside, streamlined, thin and also inscribed with the North Jewels logo. Then he felt a swift poke to the shin. He looked down at Erica. Her eyes rose to the door at the very end of the car. Her lips moved and he read two silent words. *Run! Now!*

And leave her like this? No way.

"Perfect," Mr. Grand said. "Close the case and pick it up."

Erica broke Nick's gaze. She clicked the lock closed and stood. Her shoulder shifted under the weight of the case. Her fingers tightened on the handle. Then she started counting down from ten under her breath.

Hang on. What was she doing? Counting backward was never a good thing. Under any circumstances. He felt his right eyebrow rise. She wasn't even looking at him now. Instead her silent countdown continued.

Six. Five. Four.

No! Stop!

Three. Two.

Erica!

One.

The train jolted and lurched to a stop, more suddenly than he'd expected, tossing everyone off balance and sending them stumbling.

Everyone except Erica.

Planting her feet beneath her firmly, she swung, holding the case high in both hands. She struck Mr. Grand. The gun flew from his grasp. Erica turned and pelted down the baggage car to the door that led to the rear engine.

Go time! Nick steadied himself and brought his elbow back, knocking Orson's gun away before the thug could take two steps after her. But then a cry slipped through Erica's lips as Fox caught her by the hair and dragged her back, his weapon pressed to the side of her head.

"Nice try." Mr. Grand stumbled to his feet. He touched one hand to his bleeding lips. "Looks like you're going to be more trouble than expected." He turned to Fox. "Tie them up tightly, and take the case."

The metal butt of a handgun struck Nick hard against the back of his skull. He pitched forward and the final image that filled his mind before he passed out was Erica's face locked onto his.

THREE

Consciousness returned slowly to Nick's throbbing head, starting with the shrill whine of train wheels picking up speed on the rails somewhere beneath him. The floor vibrated, shaking his body. Nick opened his eyes and saw nothing but a gap of light filtering through the murky gray darkness around him. He tried to sit up but could barely move.

He was inside some kind of box, by the feel of it. Cold metal pressed against his body beneath him, above him and in front of him. His hands were tied behind his back. His legs were bound. Panic pressed like a fist against his chest, choking the air from his lungs and making his breath shallow. Memories of spending a night in a small jail cell at the police station the night of his accident welled up inside him. He'd never done well with being trapped. He couldn't handle being confined.

Help...me, God. I need...to calm...down. He forced himself to breathe deeply, gulping in a long breath and holding it a moment before blowing it out again. *And thank You, God, they didn't gag me.* Then something soft and warm brushed against his back, filling his body with hope. He rolled over slowly, shuffling around inch by inch until he was lying on his other side.

"Nick?" Erica's voice filled the darkness. He felt her breath on his face. Her head fell against his shoulder and an unfamiliar feeling filled his chest like melted glass expanding from a glassblower's pipe.

"Erica." Her name left his mouth like a sigh. Questions flooded his mind. Where were they? How had they got there? Why did it feel like the train was speeding up when the last he remembered it had stopped? Where was Mr. Grand and his crew? But for right now, in this moment, there was only one question that burned at the top of his mind. "Are you okay? Please tell me they didn't hurt you."

"I'm fine," she said softly.

"Really?"

"Yes, really," she said. He whispered a prayer of thanksgiving into the darkness. "How about you?"

How was he now that he was breathing again, the panic had subsided and his heart had stopped pounding? Frustrated. Worried. Almost a little anxious when he thought about Zander getting caught up in all of this. The scent of her filled his senses. It was soft and gentle like lavender and pine needles, which reminded him of warm summer days and the sun pelting down as he ran through the trees from his farm to hers. She moved toward him and he felt her nestle against his chest as the train jostled them together and then apart again.

"I'm fine," he said. "Don't worry about me. Just tell me what happened. Where are we?"

"We're still in the baggage car in one of the lockers," she said. "They knocked you out and tied you up. They tied my hands behind my back and ordered me to get in here. And I did, because I figured it was best that one of us stayed conscious. Then they locked us both in."

So they hadn't wanted to kill them. They'd just wanted them alive but out of the way. Hopefully that meant that despite the size of the crew, this really was just a simple theft.

"There should be two staff in the rear engine," she said. "A conductor and an engineer. Once we get out of here, we can alert them."

And go make sure her son was okay. She hadn't said the words out loud. But somehow he could hear them loud and clear just the same.

"Zander will be okay," Nick said. "He's a tough kid."

"I know," Erica said. "He's with Tommy and Clark Lemain. They'll make sure he's okay."

"The same Clark Lemain who got busted selling both exam answers and cigarettes, and fairly successfully pinned it on me?" He didn't bother trying to hide the contempt in his voice.

"And got a full scholarship to University of Ottawa, studied law and is now the country's youngest ever Member of Provincial Parliament." Her tone of voice made it clear she'd expected him to know that. He'd always hated that tone of voice.

"Well, some people are better at hiding who they are," he said. "According to my brother, Clark had a reputation for being too handsy with girls, but no one would complain publicly. He's probably no better now. You know he had a crush on you in high school."

It was a petulant thing to say and she ignored

it. But somehow the fact that Erica was still close to a highly successful man who'd been very attracted to her galled him.

"Clark is Tommy's friend," she said. "They'll be okay."

That was the second time she'd used that word and, in his experience, he wouldn't exactly classify being with Tommy and Clark as "okay." Erica's brother had been a hothead who drank underage and would never back down from a fight. Not that Nick himself had been all that much better. Clark was a smarmy weasel who'd cultivated a nauseatingly clean-cut image while being anything but. But for now, he could keep his mouth shut on all of that. His high school years were hardly anything to crow over and he had no right to be jealous of anybody in Erica's life now.

Besides, he couldn't begin to imagine what Erica was going through and wasn't about to make things any harder on her than they already were. "How do we get out of here?"

"I don't know yet. I'm still trying to figure it out," she said. Now there was something about her tone that made the corners of his mouth curl up slightly at the edges. "The locker has a pretty standard clasp on the outside, but I've never tried to figure out how to open it from the inside."

Okay, he racked his brain for what he'd seen. He thought he could picture it. "Why does it feel like the train is speeding up?"

"Because it is," she said. Her voice shook, but only slightly, for a second. Then she seemed to grit her teeth. "The train stopped briefly, presumably in Coral Rapids, not that I could actually see out a window, then it started moving again. So hopefully that means Mr. Grand and his buddies took the case and ran."

"Why was a North Jewels Diamond Mine case sitting alone in a baggage compartment?" he asked. "I would've expected anyone transporting something that valuable to want to keep eyes on it."

"We get a lot of valuables in baggage," she said. "But on this trip, it was actually the only thing that I had to lock in the cabinet. The woman who checked it in was young, maybe early twenties. Mostly I remember she seemed kind of anxious about making sure it was secure."

"Would you recognize her again?" Nick asked. "If Mr. Grand had the combination, she might be in danger."

"Probably," she said. "I tend to pay attention to people when I check in their valuables because I have to give them a receipt and unlock the cabinet again for them at the end of the trip. But are you really okay, though? Be totally straight with me, Nick. This is no time for you to pretend you're Mr. Indestructible. They hit you pretty hard. You went down like a bag of rocks."

Well, good to know she still had his number. Truth was, everything hurt. The tight quarters and rattling wasn't helping much. But it was nothing compared to the ache in his chest when he thought about what she was going through. She'd been held at gunpoint and her child had been threatened by criminals. The last thing she needed to worry about right now was him.

"I'm okay." He felt his voice drop like someone had somehow turned it down an octave. "I promise. I'm achy, yeah. But I've been hit far worse. And thank you for double-checking."

She went quiet again and something inside told him she was thinking about Zander. He didn't know what to say. Should he reassure her again? Or ask what she was thinking? She'd always been the one who'd been good with words. He'd found it nearly impossible to even say the simplest things like "You're beautiful" or "I like you" or "You matter to me" let alone anything more about the deeper feelings growing in his heart for her back then.

He leaned forward gently and felt her forehead brush against his. Then he felt the wetness of a tear against his cheek. The Erica he'd known had always been too strong and stubborn to let herself cry in front of him. He could only remember seeing tears in her eyes once and that had been the most shameful moment of his life. They'd woken up together in the barn, with their arms around each other, and before they'd even had time to talk about their lapse in judgment, Tommy had burst in and yanked them apart. *And I'd bailed. I left her there, with her brother shouting at her, rather than standing beside her and taking the heat. I should have made it clear, then and there, how very much she mattered to me. Instead, I pretty much proved Tommy right when he accused me of not caring about her or anyone other than myself. Lord, why did I have to be so selfish and self-destructive?* The pain in his chest cranked up to eleven and suddenly his arms ached to hold her. "Oh, babe, what did they do to you?"

"I'm fine, and Erica will do." Her tone sharpened. Yeah, guess he'd forever lost the right to call her that, no matter who had a gun to their heads or what tin box they were trapped in. "They didn't lay a hand on me besides tying my hands and pushing me a bit. They told me to stay silent until the train left the station, then someone would find me eventually and I'd be reunited with my son. Now, how are we going to get our hands untied?"

He blew out a long breath and rolled slowly from one side to another and then back again. Thankfully he could feel the lump of his pocketknife still in his jacket. "If you can roll your back to me, I can position myself so that you can get my knife out of my jacket pocket and into your hands. Then we can roll back-to-back, you can pass it to me and I'll cut your hands free."

"You'll cut my hands free, in the dark, with your hands tied and your back turned?"

Well, she didn't have to sound so skeptical. Apparently in the soft haze of long-lost affection he'd managed to forget just how much she'd needled him, challenged him and pushed him. Then again, he also seemed to remember that he'd appreciated it. Sometimes.

"Yeah, Erica, I will," he said, steeling his

voice and not even trying to hide either his frustration or his determination. "Then you're going to free my hands and I'm going to use the blade to jimmy the clasp open."

He held his breath and waited for her to argue. Instead he heard something that was a cross between a sigh and "Okay" as he felt her roll over. Her hands brushed against his jacket and he guided her fingers to his pocket and waited while she eased the knife out and slid it into his hands. Then she turned her back to him.

"Just don't cut me," she said.

"I'm not planning on it." In fact, he was praying very hard that he wouldn't. He opened the pocketknife, tapped his finger against the tip to make sure it was pointing the right direction and started to carefully cut the rope binding her wrists. Silence fell in the space between them, a silence that he wanted to fill with words he didn't know how to speak.

"So you finally met Zander," she said after a long moment.

"I did," he said. There was a weight to her words that he couldn't quite decipher. "I… I had no idea you had a child."

He felt her freeze. Tension seemed to radiate

down her arms and limbs and into her hands. Had he said something wrong? He had so many questions. Starting with who Zander's father was. Not that he had the right to ask.

"How did you meet Zander?" she asked, and it was only then he realized she didn't know how they'd ended up in the dining car.

"He found me, woke me up and asked me for my help," Nick told her. "He said he'd seen bad guys with guns under the table in the dining car and wanted me to help him rescue you. He was very insistent."

A small gasp slipped through her lips and he had the distinct impression that whatever she'd been about to say she'd bitten back.

"In fact, he tried to talk me into letting him have my gun," he added.

She laughed. It was a watery laugh that seemed half laugh and half sob.

They lapsed back into silence and he was surprised at how quickly he missed the sound of her voice. He didn't know what to say. Or even what he wanted to. That she'd been everything to him when they'd been younger, but he'd never really felt worthy of her affection. Of anyone's love really.

He'd been born into an amazing, incredibly

strong, God-loving family. But he also never remembered a time when he hadn't looked at his sister's picture on the wall and wondered if his birth had felt like some kind of consolation prize. He'd never quite understood why his family's tragedy had made him want to act out, shove back, be a brat and generally try to see just how far he could push people away before they stopped loving him. His parents, his brothers and God had never given up on him. But while Erica had patiently stood by him for years, he'd eventually pushed her one step too far.

I cared about her the most, Lord. So why did I treat her the worst? Why did I refuse to even call her my girlfriend when that's clearly what she was? Why did I have to blow everything up to see just how much she mattered to me?

Because he had. Because he did. And, generally, he was thankful for everything that mistake had changed in his life. How it had pushed him to be a better, stronger and faithful man. He'd even tried dating a couple of women on base and being the gentleman who Erica had deserved. But it had never worked. No one, no matter how nice a person, had ever been her.

He gritted his teeth and focused on the job at hand.

"I can't stop wondering what happened to the other train staff," Erica said eventually, after a very long moment of silence. "There are supposed to be eight of us. Two engineers, two conductors and four train attendants. And Bob Bass is driving the engine today. We normally have a larger crew for the day shift, but the night train runs on a skeletal crew. The staff tend to congregate in two groups at opposite ends of the train, in the front and rear engines, this late at night. But still, we should've seen someone, and they should've seen what was happening on the security cameras."

"What's a rear engine?"

"Exactly same as a front engine, it just points in the opposite direction. It means we can change direction without turning around and make the entire trip without refueling. Either one of them can drive the train. It's like a snake with a head at both ends." He felt her shrug and grabbed her wrists with his fingers to steady them again.

"Trains are pretty soundproof," she told him, "because they're all individual cars. Add in the noise of the train and the rain outside, you could probably fire a gun in one car and all you'd hear in the other would be a muffled bang like something falling over. Especially if it had a silencer."

Not exactly comforting. His hand slipped, taking the blade with it. She winced. So did he. "Did I hurt you?"

"Just pricked me. Only a little. It's okay. You can keep going."

He ran his fingers over the rope. He'd cut through enough that it had begun to fray and the blade was too close to her skin for his liking. He set the knife down and started to pull the rope apart strand by strand. She sighed. He knew that sound. "Don't worry," he said. "You'll be free in a moment, you'll be reunited with your son and this will all be over soon. I promise."

For a long moment neither of them said anything. They just lay there back-to-back, the heels of her leather shoes brushing against the backs of his legs as the train rumbled through the night beneath them. Finally he felt the rope fall free from her hands and heard her gasp in relief. Then he felt her roll over and pick up the knife. She started cutting his hands free. The fact that her hands were free and she could actually face him would make it go much faster now.

"You really didn't know about Zander?" Her voice moved behind him in the darkness. Why was she bringing this up again? Should he have?

"No," he admitted. "I really didn't."

"Tommy said he told you when I was pregnant," she said. "Plus, Huntsville is a very small town." Her voice trailed off and he had the impression there were words she was keeping herself from saying.

"It's not that small," he said. "Plus, I'd joined the army and you'd moved to Kingston. Basically, Tommy told me that you'd left town and were better off without me."

"Well, I didn't know you were in the army."

The rope snapped from his hands. For a second he just lay there, too stunned to know what to say and fighting the urge to turn toward her. Instead he took the knife from her hands, brought it around in front of him and slid the blade into the tiny gap of light. He started working on popping the clasp open. "How could you not know I was in the army?"

"You said it yourself. I'd moved to Kingston for university and you'd moved on base."

"Yes, but I wrote you a letter! Telling you I'd joined the army. Telling you…everything."

The clasp snapped back. The door fell open. Light flooded through. He rolled out, stood and then reached back for her. But Erica was already crawling out of the locker. Her auburn hair had slipped from its braid and now fell in messy loose waves around her face. His mouth went dry. She ignored his hand and pushed herself to her feet.

"Well, if you sent me a letter, I didn't get it. I blocked both your cell phone number and your email address. You can't really blame me for that."

"I didn't. I don't. But I wrote you an actual physical letter—a really long one, with pen and paper—and hand delivered it to your house."

She opened her mouth. But before she could speak, a shout came from the other end of the baggage car. He looked up. The door flew open. Fox ran through, a gun in his hands.

"Get behind me!" Nick shouted, throwing himself between her and the charging criminal. "And stay down!"

She dropped to the ground and rolled, even as she heard the sound of the gun firing and a bullet flying over her head. It clanged against the ceiling and ricocheted. She sprang to her feet, ran for the door, yanked it open and tumbled into the gap between the cars. Then she yanked on the handle of the door leading to the rear engine. It was locked. Why was it locked?

"It's Erica Knight! Let me in." Desperately, she banged on the window and pounded the door. No sound, no motion. Nothing came from behind the glass. "Come on! Somebody! Let me in!"

A second bullet sounded. She hit the floor and rolled. The reinforced window of the rear engine door—the one she'd been banging on just seconds before—cracked into a web of glass. She turned around, trapped in the no-man's-land between two train cars, with Nick and Fox battling on one side and a locked door on the other. She slid her body against the wall, looked around the corner and watched as Nick threw himself at Fox. They wrestled for the gun. Her heart leaped into her throat as she watched Nick's strong, lean form battle to rip the weapon away from a man twice his size.

Help me, Lord!

She had to think. She had to act. But one thought seemed to pound through her like a strong and relentless heartbeat as she watched the soldier and the thief exchange blows. *That soldier was Nick!* The boy she'd loved, longed for, hated and lost, was back. He'd always been athletic. But now he was brave. He was courageous. He was the kind of man who'd throw himself in the path of a criminal's gun after giving his helmet and bulletproof vest to her son. *Their son.* The son Nick clearly had known nothing about. She never should've trusted Tommy. Then again, denying the baby was his and bailing had seemed like the kind of thing the Nick she'd known would do. She had to tell him. He had to know.

But not here. Not now.

"Erica!" Nick shouted. "Get ready to catch!"

Catch what? She leaned around the corner just in time to watch as Nick delivered a quick and swift uppercut to Fox's jaw, knocking him back so hard the gun flew from his hand and skidded across the ground. Nick dived for it. Fox lunged after him, catching Nick around the legs and sending him sprawling to the ground. Nick's hand shot out, flicking the gun and sending it flying down the metal floor toward her. She darted out from behind the door and scrambled for it.

Fox looked up. His cold dark eyes met hers. He charged at her. Nick caught him by the shoulder and yanked him back.

"Get to the rear engine!" Nick shouted. "I'll catch up with you."

The engine door was still locked! She ran back into the space between the cars.

"Get back!" she shouted to whoever might be listening inside the rear engine. "I'm going to try to shoot out the window!"

She stepped as far as she could to the side and prayed she was far enough out of the line of fire to avoid getting hit by broken glass or a ricocheting bullet. Then she raised the gun, aimed at the splintered window and fired twice. The first bullet bent the reinforced glass pane inward. The second destroyed what remained of the window. She yanked her decorative uniform scarf from around her neck, wrapped it around her hand, stuck it through the window and unlocked the door from the inside. She forced the door open and tumbled into the rear engine, praying with every heartbeat that Nick would be just one step behind her. Glass crackled beneath her feet. Her heart pounded so hard she could barely breathe. "We have to stop the train and alert the authorities. There are armed thieves on board!"

She froze. There was no one there. The engine car was empty. She grabbed the phone from the wall and was greeted with a dull emptiness of silence. She lunged for the radio. It was down, too. She considered using the internal walkie-talkies she used to communicate with other train staff, but it was hardly private and anyone with a walkie-talkie on the right channel could listen in. Then a flicker of motion caught her eyes. The security cameras were still on, scrolling through the camera feeds, showing her row upon row of sleeping passengers and the empty dining car. Then the first-class lounge area flickered into view.

There, in black and white, was a small, unmistakable form curled into Tommy's side-sleeper chair. Her breath caught in her throat. *Zander.* He was still in Nick's helmet and bulletproof vest. It looked like Zander and his uncle were quietly playing cars together, while Clark sat on the sleeper chair opposite with his head in his hands and Mr. Grand and Lou stood armed by the door.

Lord, keep him safe until we figure out a

way to get him out of there and back into my arms safely.

There was a bang, loud and deafening, like thunder and lightning crashing inside the train behind her. She turned just in time to see the rear engine door crash open. She spun back with her hands raised. It was Nick.

"It's done," he said. "He's been neutralized. I bound his hands, gagged his mouth and put him in the same place he'd put us. It seemed like the most humane, kind way to deal with him until we can get help and call the authorities. I also locked the baggage door from the inside and shoved one of the storage lockers in front of it. So, basically, we're barricaded in. Really hoping there's some way we can call the authorities from in here. Also, when I did a weapons check, I found two knives, a gun and also a dummy weapon. Why he'd be carrying both a real and a fake replica gun is beyond me."

What? It was beyond her, too.

Nick's eyes widened. "What's wrong?"

"The phone's dead…" She took a breath, somehow finding the next thing she needed to tell him so hard to say that her mouth didn't want to form the words.

"And?" Nick asked.

"They never got off the train. Mr. Grand and his gang of thieves still have Zander…"

"Oh, Erica. I'm so sorry."

Compassion flooded his green eyes. He glanced past her to the security camera feed. Then his gaze returned to her face. He stood there for one long moment, just looking at her. He ran his hand over his head as if feeling for the shaggy hair that was no longer there. His mouth opened, then closed as he shrugged as if failing to find words. And all of a sudden it was like she was looking through time at the old Nick, the boy who'd been her best friend, the boy she'd loved with all her youthful heart.

Suddenly she found herself running toward him. His arms parted, and she tumbled into his chest. His arms slid around her. She heard a simple and short prayer for God's help and guidance murmured under his breath. Then she felt his hand stroke the back of her head. "Don't worry. We'll rescue Zander. We'll get help. It'll all be okay. I promise."

"No, don't say that." She shook her head. He'd promised he'd always be there for her the night she'd fallen into his arms. But the moment her overprotective brother had shown up and stared yelling, Nick had bailed. "Don't make promises you don't know you can keep."

She pressed her palms into his chest and pushed him back, gasping like she'd come up for air. He let her go. She turned away from him and ran her hands over her eyes. She hadn't fought long and hard to build a life for her and Zander to fall into a man's arms and expect him to protect her.

Especially not if that man was Nick Henry.

Nick cleared his throat. She knew that sound. It was the sound he'd always made when gearing up to say something emotional, as if he had to summon the courage to find the words to say anything real. Then she'd always wait, her hopes up, as he'd stumble through half a sentence before deflecting, making a silly joke and changing the subject. Well, this time, whatever he had to say, she wasn't going to stand around and wait.

She rolled her shoulders back and turned toward the monitors.

"The phone is down," she said, forcing out words to keep the anxiety at bay. "Which means we're going to have to hope that somebody on this train has a satellite phone. I know it's a total long shot because they're very expensive and rare. But a regular cell phone won't cut it. We'll never get a cell signal up here. Like I said, the criminals have not left the train, the train staff is still missing, and my son is still in danger. Thankfully some of the security cameras seem to be working. The system only lets you scroll back about half an hour. But if we watch, we can get a better idea of what exactly happened on this train. Hang on."

Her fingers moved over the controls. This was good. This was something practical she could do, something she could control. She didn't have the front engine or the dining car, but she could scroll through the economy cars and watch as passengers slept and stretched.

"Are there cameras in the sleeper cabins?" Nick asked after a long moment.

"No, only in the first-class lounge."

"Where are the other first-class passengers?"

"Besides Mr. Grand and his crew, Clark was the only other person who booked a first-class ticket, which isn't unheard-of at this time of year," she said. "He apparently had some big meeting up North and so asked Tommy if he wanted to bring Zander up with him. Said it might be fun for Zander to get to see his mommy at work. Hang on…"

She watched as Mr. Grand approached another one of the train attendants in the economy car and pressed a gun into his side. One by one, Mr. Grand or one of his thugs stalked her coworkers, waiting until the train staffer was isolated and alone and then pointed a gun at them and escorted them into one of the first-class car's sleeper cabins. What Nick had said about Fox carrying a fake replica gun flashed through her mind. Were all these weapons real? Had all the weapons that had been aimed at her in the dining car been real? The one Fox had fired at them most certainly had been.

It was like watching a slowly unfolding black-and-white horror movie, as the two conductors, the rear engineer and the other three attendants were rounded up and led into one of the cars, terrified, forced to their knees, their mouths gagged and their hands bound. Why? What was he going to do to them? Then she watched as a slender, dark-haired passenger was roused from her seat by Julie, who it seemed was asking her for some kind of help. Julie led the woman into the dining car, where Rowan and Mr. Grand met her at gunpoint.

"I'm pretty sure that's the woman who checked in the North Jewels Diamond Mine laptop."

Erica's voice fell silent as questions she didn't want to ask filled her mind. Then she watched on the playback as the train stopped and Mr. Grand ordered them to walk single file out the door and into the night. Through the gap in the open door captured by the camera, she watched as they fell to their knees on the ground, in the rain and the darkness. The door closed. The train went on its way.

No. Please, Lord, no...

She turned to Nick.

"The train stopped," she said as the full impact of what she'd seen washed like cold water over her limbs. "But not at Coral Rapids. It stopped a days' walk from the nearest town. Somewhere with no roads or electricity. He tied up my colleagues, forced them out of the train and left them stranded, without food or coats or any way to get help, in the middle of nowhere."

FOUR

In an instant, she felt Nick's strong hand on her back, between her shoulder blades, like a backstop.

"They'll be okay," Nick said. "They'll get themselves untied. They'll find shelter in the woods. The storm will stop eventually. They've got rainwater to drink and the human body can survive weeks without food. All they have to do is stay by the tracks. Rescue teams will search for them and find them."

"But how long will it take?" she said. "Nobody knows we're in danger. Nobody knows they're out there. They cooperated, exactly like I did, and were forced off a train in the middle of nowhere."

She'd agreed to take them to the baggage compartment and get the case. She'd agreed to leave Zander in Tommy and Clark's care. She hadn't struggled when they'd bound her hands, and agreed to crawl into the storage locker. What if he'd forced her off the train without Zander? Or him off the train without her?

"Does this mean you're the only member of the train crew left on board?" Nick asked.

"The only person I didn't see them order off the train is Bob Bass, the front engineer."

"Maybe they needed somebody to drive the train?" Nick suggested.

"Probably," she said. "But if I'd been planning on hijacking a train, I'd be sure to bring someone with me who could drive one."

"You would." Nick chuckled softly. "Is Bob a good man? Could he be in on the heist? Is he open to being bribed or blackmailed?"

"Maybe," she said. "He's lazy and crass. He shows up late, overshoots the platform and tells inappropriate jokes, stuff like that. But I'm going to assume he's being held hostage and forced to drive the train until I know otherwise."

She watched until the cameras caught up to real time, then switched back to live feed.

"I'm done cooperating," she said. "I took Mr. Grand to the case and unlocked the cabinet for him because railway policy is to de-escalate

the situation and put people's lives above anything else. But as far as I'm concerned, policy
no longer applies. Right now the only thing that
matters is keeping everyone on this train safe."

Especially Zander. And if there was even
the smallest possibility that telling Nick he was
Zander's father would lead to him running off,
half-cocked, doing something reckless and stupid, then that would have to wait. Zander was a
part of her. Her impetuous, little bundle of en-
ergy that had seemingly exploded into the life
she had planned for herself, turning it upside
down and sending it down a whole new track.
The camera feed scrolled, the first-class cabin
appeared. Her finger slid up against the screen.

*Don't worry, Little Soldier. I'm coming to
save you with the help of the soldier you were
so smart to find to help. Who's also your daddy.*

She heard Nick clear his throat again. She
turned, but his eyes scanned past her, their
green depths searching the screen. His voice
deepened. "You're right that I shouldn't make
promises I don't know I can keep. But I can
promise I will do absolutely everything in my
power to protect your child, Erica. I promise."

Our child.

The words wrenched inside her like someone had physically taken her heart and twisted it. It wasn't right to keep the truth from him, even if she was worried telling him would make things worse. "Nick, there's something I have to tell you—"

"Me, too." He grabbed both her hands and squeezed them. "Let me go first."

"No." She shook her head.

"Yes—"

"This can't wait—"

"Erica, I am so incredibly sorry for how I treated you," he said, blurting the words out so quickly it was like he was tumbling down a hill, kicking words up as he went. "You deserved so much better than me. You were the best person I've ever known. You were kind and sweet and caring. You were there for me and listened to me. You gave me an opportunity to grow up and be a better man. And I wasted it. I blew it. You deserved a better man than me. I'm just so sorry I wasn't him."

"Nick, I—"

A buzzing sound took over the air, like an unseen mosquito or the distant murmur of voices, the sound cutting off the swelling of whatever it was she felt building like a balloon inside her chest. Then she heard a voice, too faint to make out the words.

"That's the walkie-talkie receiver!" She dropped his hand. "We have it set to low volume so internal chatter between the train attendants doesn't disturb the engineer." She turned up the volume on the receiver and grabbed a walkie-talkie to reply. She pressed the button, trying to block out the feeling of Nick's shoulder brushing against hers as he leaned in. "Hello?"

"Erica Knight?" Mr. Grand's voice dripped like a melting icicle down the line. "I see you made it out of the locker. And as you can clearly see on the monitors, I still have your friend, brother and your son. So when you're done holding hands with your soldier friend, how about we discuss just how much your son's life means to you and what you're willing to do to keep him safe?"

Mr. Grand could see them! The thought pounded through Nick's mind as he scanned the rear engine for the security cameras. Sure enough, two small black orbs sat on either end of the car. He could've kicked himself. Why hadn't he thought of that before? Why hadn't Erica?

Because she was worried about her son.

He couldn't blame her. If he ever had a child, and that child was in danger, no power on earth would be able to stop Nick from getting to him. Including logic.

"What do you want?" Erica asked, her voice every bit as calm and steady as her hands had been back at the shooting range when he'd taught her how to shoot a target.

"You are going to stop playing games and come here," Mr. Grand said.

"Why didn't you leave the train?" Fear battled defiance in her face. "You got what you wanted."

Mr. Grand let out a noise somewhere between a cough and a laugh that contained neither mirth nor warmth. It reminded Nick of an irritated rattlesnake.

"Come here," Mr. Grand snapped. "Now!"

A shiver ran down Nick's spine. There was a quake of frustration in the thief's voice. For the first time since he'd encountered Mr. Grand, he had absolutely no doubt that his mask was slipping and his real feelings were leaking through. The man was frustrated. Nick suspected that he had definitely planned to leave the train but something in his plan had changed or something had gone wrong. *But what? And what did it mean?*

"You have one of my men locked in the storage compartment," Mr. Grand said. "You will go set him free, return his weapon to him and walk with him through the train to me, nice and slowly. You will not do anything to alert anyone that anything is wrong. Is that clear? Otherwise..."

The sentence ended with threats that made Nick's blood boil as Mr. Grand's words grew ugly and vile. But Erica's eyes turned to Nick. And despite the wall of pain and doubt he'd thrown up between them, somehow there was still that same something there that had kept drawing his heart and mind deeper toward hers, no matter how many times he'd pushed her away.

Fierce determination shone like firelight reflected on her face. Just how impossibly strong was this woman? Her child had been kidnapped. Her brother and his friend were being held hostage. She'd been threatened at gunpoint. Her colleagues had been ordered off the train and stranded in the middle of nowhere. But here she was, still standing, still holding it together, still trying to find a way out. And for a fleeting moment it hit him that maybe, just maybe, she'd have been strong enough to forgive him if he hadn't given up on them, after he'd blown up what they'd had and smashed it to smithereens.

"Yeah," Erica said when Mr. Grand took a pause in his swear words and threats. "We've got it. You want us to get your guy, bring him to you and not alert any of the passengers or anyone else on the train that anything is wrong."

She said the last few words with added emphasis, as if saying them for Nick's benefit. Yeah, he'd caught that, too. Despite the size of his crew, it didn't seem taking a whole train hostage was Mr. Grand's plan. That would almost be comforting if it wasn't for the chilling reminder in the form of the rest of the crew being forced out into the night that Mr. Grand meant business.

"Come alone!" Mr. Grand barked. "Just you."

Alone? But then how could he protect her? How could he have her back?

"But I need his help to—"

"You. Will. Come. Alone!" Mr. Grand's voice rose. "If I so much as see that soldier step one foot beyond the baggage car, I'll shoot a hostage. You have exactly fifteen minutes to free my associate and get here or I start shooting people. Have I made myself clear?"

Nick turned to Erica, his eyes pleading. She could not agree to go alone to the criminal, without him. She just couldn't.

But Erica didn't answer. Instead she just stood there, the walkie-talkie in her hand, shaking slightly. Her gaze rose to the ceiling.

"Erica?" Nick squeezed her fingers. "Are you all right?"

Erica's head shook. Her hand went limp in his. The walkie-talkie began to slide from her hand.

"I'm in charge here!" Mr. Grand shouted. "You got that? I have all the power. I'm the one holding the gun and holding the people you care about hostage. You are nothing but a train waitress."

Erica's body crumpled suddenly, like a marionette whose strings had just been cut. The walkie-talkie fell from her hand. She collapsed to the floor.

FIVE

"Erica!" Something lurched in Nick's chest. He dropped to the floor beside her crumpled body. He could still hear Mr. Grand's muffled voice shouting threats into the walkie-talkie. But all that mattered was the woman now curled on the ground. Why had he believed she was strong enough to take this? He was the military corporal, not her. He crouched low and brushed his hand across her face. "Erica... are you okay?"

"Nick, I'm fine." Despite the fact she was lying on the floor, her voice was as strong and steady as steel. "Don't move. Just stay here."

"What? No." He pushed back and started to pull away, but then, to his surprise, she threw her arms around him.

"Stop!" she whispered. "Just hold me. Wrap

your arms around me and whatever you do, don't look up."

She was holding on to him so tightly it was like he'd got too close to the edge of a lifeboat and she was trying to keep him from falling out. Her hands slipped up around his neck, her head buried deeply in the crook of his neck. He'd forgotten the way her body fitted so perfectly against his chest.

"Listen," she whispered. Her mouth so close to his face that her breath tickled his ear. "He's watching us and we've only got a few moments before he figures out something is up. So we've got to talk now and talk fast."

"Got it," he said. "Do the cameras have audio?"

"No, but he can clearly see our faces. I don't want him to think we're whispering or conspiring."

So she'd pretended to collapse to buy them a few moments. Smart move. Still, Nick could feel the urge to leap to his feet and take action boiling up inside him like a pot about to flip its lid. Instead he took a deep breath and prayed. *Okay, God. Let me hold tight and listen. I owe her that much at least.*

"You can't agree to his demands," he said.

"You can't walk up there alone with some armed thug."

He felt her stiffen. "I don't like it any more than you do," she said. "But let's put a pin in that for now, because I'm not sure what other options we have."

"Can we stop the train?"

"Not from here." She shook her head. Her soft hair brushed against his face. "We'd have to make it to the front engine."

"Is there some way to cut off the fuel supply?"

"Not easily from a moving train and even if there was, the engines run everything. We'd have to think about what kind of situation we'd be stranding passengers in."

"Yeah, but that's better than being on a moving train controlled by hijackers—"

"It's not like sitting in a car with the engine off," Erica said. "Don't you remember the huge train disaster where someone turned the train's engines off, the brakes stopped doing their job, the train rolled, derailed and destroyed a large part of the town? The last thing we want is a runaway train falling off a bridge into a lake."

"Okay, fine, we don't cut the engine—"

"We could separate the train," she said.

"Then this would become a new front engine and we could go south, back to safety, without having to turn around. But we'd need to get to Bob. We need his help for that. And there's no way we could separate the train until Zander's safely with me. The idea of him and Tommy going on in the front half of the train while we escape to safety is unthinkable. I think the best option is if I go join my son and you stay here and search the baggage car for anything you can use to contact the outside world. Flares or a satellite phone would be nice."

He'd thought they were putting a pin in the idea of her agreeing to Mr. Grand's demands and being taken hostage without him. "I don't want you going alone—"

"You want to be taken hostage?" she asked. "Because, trust me, I don't. But if I can't contact the outside world, get help or rescue Zander, then I'd rather be taken hostage alongside my little boy, so that he's not going through this without me. And you're strong enough and a good enough fighter to evade Fox when he takes me. Hide somewhere. Barricade yourself in somewhere. Let him tie you up and then escape. I don't care how you do it. But our best option is for me to join my son and you to plan a rescue from the outside. And, knowing you, I think you'd rather be out here, plotting and planning something—anything—than be held hostage in a room with us."

She might be right about that. But for the first time in his life Nick wasn't actually sure. He could hear the faint sound of Mr. Grand shouting now. They were down to their final few seconds. He gritted his teeth. "I'll stay behind. I'll look for weapons and I'll also try to recruit some other passengers. If my work with the Canadian Rangers has taught me anything, it's that other people are our greatest strengths in a crisis."

Something told him that the private security guy might not like the idea of being taken hostage. The elderly gentleman with military bearing and his diminutive wife crossed Nick's mind, too.

"I definitely don't want to involve passengers." Erica's voice sharpened. "Under any circumstances."

"Well, neither do I," he said. "But we don't have a ton of options—"

"Or facts," she interrupted. "What was it you taught me about not trying to shoot at a target before you see it? We don't know why Mr.

Grand assembled a crew of six people to steal a case from North Jewels Diamond Mine, why they ordered almost all of the staff off the train or what they're planning to do when they get to Moosonee. But my hunch is that Mr. Grand's plan doesn't actually involve holding a whole train hostage."

He felt her body start to pull away. "I should go."

Now it was his turn to hold her fast. "Look, I hate to say this—"

"Then don't—"

"But what's the possibility that Tommy has something to do with this?" Nick plowed on.

"Tommy wouldn't do anything of the sort!"

"It would explain why you weren't ordered off the train, and why he, Zander and Clark have been kept safe," Nick argued.

"So would the fact that they're traveling in a private sleeper cabin with a prominent politician," she shot back. "Maybe Mr. Grand's plans changed when he realized just who he'd taken hostage. A well-known face is a better bargaining chip in a potential hostage situation. Or maybe Clark smooth-talked Mr. Grand to keep Tommy and Zander safe with some kind of bribe. I'd even be more willing to believe Clark had something to do with this than Tommy did. Clark's always been a sleaze who managed to con people into believing he was a better man than he was." Unlike him, Nick thought, who'd preferred to wear his flaws like armor. "But not Tommy. My brother might have his problems. He had a few minor brushes with the law when he was younger and has racked up a lot of debts. But he has a good heart and would never actually hurt anybody."

"He once punched me in the face."

"Do you really want to argue over who punched who and where?" she asked. "You both got into a lot of stupid fights back then! Especially when you were drinking! I'm just thankful neither of you ever got seriously hurt!"

Except for the damage he'd done to himself by crashing Max's car.

"I didn't say I was a good guy back then!" They definitely did not have time for this. But then again, Nick couldn't exactly discount the possibility that the first thing Fox would do when released would be to shoot Nick in the head. This might be the last conversation they ever had. And if so, was this really how he wanted it to go?

"I said I was sorry and I meant it. I'm sure

you wish there was somebody other than me here in your corner right now. But I'm telling you, if I was in your shoes, and my kid was in danger, no force on earth would stop me from doing whatever it took to save him. And, if given the opportunity, I'd do the same for you."

There was a long pause, longer than he liked, punctuated only by the rattle of the train, the pounding of the rain above them and the faint shouts of Mr. Grand trying to drag their attention back to the walkie-talkie. He whispered a prayer under his breath, asking God to keep them, Zander and everyone else safe and alive.

Erica whispered, "Amen," and it was only then that his arms loosened.

"You have some pretty impressive grip strength, by the way," he said, suddenly desperate to say something, anything, to deflect from the fact she was about to let herself be taken hostage. He stood slowly, then reached for her hand. "Zander says you pack a mean punch."

"I do kickboxing," she said. She took his hand. "Thanks for getting me into it."

He pulled her up. "Miss hitting me?"

"Maybe." A faint smile curled her lips. "Did you miss sparring with me?"

"I missed kissing you."

Her eyes widened. *Yeah, probably shouldn't have said that.* She stood there for a heartbeat, her hand still in his. Then suddenly she leaned forward, her lips brushed against his so quickly he barely had a moment to register that she'd just kissed him and he'd kissed her back. She pulled back and reached for the walkie-talkie. "See you later, Nick."

"Enough stalling. I'm done being patient." Mr. Grand's tone came down the line, hard and coarse and furious. "We're doing it my way and we're doing it now... You! Come with me," Mr. Grand's voice seemed suddenly fainter on the line and it took Nick a moment to realize that he was talking to somebody other than him. They watched on the screen as Mr. Grand waved his gun at Clark, who stumbled to his feet, and Tommy said something Nick couldn't quite catch.

But Clark's response echoed down the line. "No worries, man. It's going to be fine. I'll be right back. Just take care of your lovely sister and nephew."

They watched on the monitors as Mr. Grand led him out, the door to the first-class cabin closing behind him.

"Where did they go? I can't see them." Erica's free hand reached for Nick's arm. Her fingers slid down his sleeve until they reached his hand. His fingers linked through hers.

Then the camera changed. Mr. Grand and Clark were standing alone in the dining car.

"I warned you that if you didn't do exactly as I said, I was going to start shooting people. This is on you." Mr. Grand pointed the gun at the politician's head. "Kneel."

Clark's eyes rose to the camera, as if he knew they were there. His chin rose bravely. He held the camera's gaze like a man facing a firing squad, like a man who knew he was about to die.

Nick felt Erica's fingers shake.

"No!" Erica's shouted. "Don't do this! I'll do what you say. Just let Clark go. Nobody else has to die."

"This is not a trade!" Mr. Grand's voice rose. "This is a warning. Now, say goodbye."

He held the walkie-talkie to Clark's ear.

"Hey, Erica?" The politician's voice was as smooth as ever with only a quiver of fear. "I guess we're never going to end up going for that coffee, after all. If I'd known it was going to go down like this, I'd have come up with some great final last words. Something like 'be good to each other' and 'love your country.'"

"Don't be ridiculous," Erica said. "He's bluffing."

"Take care of yourself and your son," Clark said. "It was a pleasure knowing you."

Mr. Grand fired.

Clark crumpled to the ground.

Unshed tears flooded Erica's eyes as she watched Mr. Grand drag Clark's limp body out of the dining car and back into one of the first-class cabins.

"I'm sorry," Nick said, but it seemed like his voice was coming from somewhere very far away. "He didn't deserve that."

No, Clark hadn't. Nobody did. And yet here they all were, caught in some nightmare of somebody else's creation.

"It's all my fault." Her shoulders shook. "If it wasn't for me…" Her voice trailed off.

"Don't say that." Nick took her by the shoulders and turned her to face him. But she couldn't lift her head to meet his eyes. "None of this is your fault. None! For all we know, this is a professional hit to take out a politician and the case is just a distraction."

She doubted it and suspected Nick was just saying it to make her feel better. Her hands brushed his arms, feeling the strength of him under her fingertips. "Let's go. Just...don't let them kill you."

He chuckled softly, sadly. "I wasn't planning on it."

Lord, help me reach my son. Help me get him out of here safely. Zander's all that matters in my life.

She stumbled into the baggage compartment, her unshed tears like a wall of water obstructing her view. Ahead, she could barely see as Nick let Fox out of his compartment, returned his weapon to him and told him that Mr. Grand wanted Fox and Erica to come see him in first class. The soldier shoved the storage locker that he'd used to block the baggage car door aside. Fox delivered a swift blow to the back of Nick's head. Nick crumpled to the ground and Fox raised his weapon, as if ready to deliver another blow when Nick leaped to his feet. But Nick lay still. Fox snorted, grabbed Erica tightly by the arm and shoved the gun hard into her side. Her body was so numb she barley felt it. "Walk."

They walked forward.

Clark Lemain was dead. Sure, he'd been

pushy, with too high an opinion of himself, and had a habit of making proprietary comments about Zander needing a father. But he was a person, he was her brother's friend, she'd known him since kindergarten and now he was dead. Mr. Grand had taken his first life and it was because of her.

Her heart pounded with thoughts too painful to put into words. Her colleagues had been tied up and left in the middle of nowhere in the rain. Her brother's friend had died. There was nothing to stop her or Zander from the next people killed. *Lord, help me. Please. I don't even know what to pray right now.*

She half expected someone to be waiting for them on the other side of the door. Instead, there was no one there. Fox led her out of the baggage car and everything inside her wanted to look back at the soldier—her soldier, her Nick—lying there on the baggage car floor. But if she did, those tears would start falling and she'd never stop crying. She'd collapse like she had the night Nick had taken her heart in his hand and smashed it to shards. She'd spent days in her room, crying and shouting, feeling weak and helpless, blaming herself, until the relentless sickness in her stomach revealed itself to be more than depression and a broken heart. It was a baby. His baby. Their baby. She was going to have a child. That was the day she got up, washed her face and decided her child needed her to be strong and to stop feeling sorry for herself.

At least this time she'd let herself kiss Nick goodbye. And she had to believe that soon, in the future, when they were all safe and all the dust had settled, and she told Nick that Zander was his son, he'd understand why she'd waited. Nick would be just as dedicated to protecting Zander if he didn't know and far less likely to go off like a loose cannon if she suddenly sprang the news on him. And Zander's safety was all she was going to focus on now.

She stepped slowly, focusing on keeping one foot in front of the other as she and Fox walked through the passenger cars toward the front of the train. Around her, passengers slept, or at least looked like they were trying to. Seemed she'd been right in suspecting that the sound of a gunshot wouldn't have carried through the train, especially since Grand had used a silencer. Rain lashed the darkened windows. The stench of cigarettes on Fox's breath came inches from her face. She kept her eyes straight ahead as they passed from the first passenger car through the connecting space and into another, then slowly through that one into the next.

The ground dragged beneath her feet suddenly, jolting her mind awake, as if she'd been sleepwalking. The train was slowing beneath her, in the middle of nowhere, with no station around for miles, and yet she could feel it, through the soles of her shoes. The train was stopping.

"Keep moving." Fox's grip tightened on her arm. "What's going on?"

"It's not me. It's the train."

The people around her could feel it, too. Their eyes were blinking. They were shifting in their seats. Any moment now and they'd be getting to their feet, asking why the train had stopped and realizing soon enough that almost all of the staff was gone. Whoever was stopping the train here, now, in the middle of nowhere, and whatever they thought they were doing, they were about to make everyone's situation a whole lot more dangerous.

A cough dragged her attention to her right. A broad man in a dark blazer, surrounded by other men in business suits, flickered his eyes in her direction for a moment. Then she felt a boot, swift and precise, kicking her in the back of the knee and buckling her leg. She pitched forward, falling away from Fox's grasp as she tumbled onto her hands and knees on the floor of the train. A smattering of voices gasped. Okay, people were really waking up now. She looked back. Had the man in a blazer really tripped her? The stranger's eyes searched her face with an inscrutable look that made it impossible to tell if he was friend or foe. But somehow oddly reminded her of Nick's brothers in law enforcement.

Who was he? Had he tripped her on purpose? And if so, what reason could he possibly have for that? Yes, he'd momentarily got her a few feet away from Fox's gun, but if he'd suspected something was wrong, or wanted to confirm Fox was holding a gun on her, this was a really weird way to respond to it.

But any attempt to get an answer to that was suddenly put on hold as her attention was suddenly drawn to movement in the window at the end of the train car. A face, impossibly handsome, infuriating and strong, met hers through the glass. *Nick!* He'd followed, creeping behind them as they'd moved from car to car. She should've known Fox's blow hadn't been strong enough to take a man that hardheaded down. She also should've known Nick wasn't going to stay behind like agreed. No, instead he was going to be impulsive. Instead he was going to risk getting somebody else killed.

She caught his gaze and held it. Hard.

No, Nick. No. Trust me. Whatever you're thinking of doing right now, don't do it.

Fox kicked her in the side. He jabbed the gun so deeply into the pocket of his open jacket she could clearly see the outline. "Get up! Walk! Now!"

"Hey, lady?" The blazered man stood and stretched. "Is everything okay? You took quite a fall."

Like he hadn't been the person who'd tripped her.

"Hey!" Fox spun toward him. "She's with me."

"Is that all right with you, miss?" The man crossed large arms over a broad chest. Dark eyes, under darker brows, fixed on Erica. "Or would you like to sit down and join us for a bit?"

"How about you sit down and mind your business!" Fox yanked the gun from his pocket.

Passengers gasped. The man's hands rose. But it was the unmistakable rhythm of the jolt of the train beneath her—hard forward, hard back—that made Erica's heart leap into her throat.

Oh, no, no, no, no, no, no...

The train wasn't just stopping. It was separating.

SIX

"Erica! Get down!" Nick's voice was loud behind her.

She dropped to the floor and looked back just in time to see Nick lunge through the door. The thief turned on Nick and fired. But Nick was too fast, dropping to the floor and rolling beneath the bullet as it flew past him out of the car. Passengers screamed and ducked behind the seats. Nick leaped to his feet, swung his elbow back and leveled a blow at Fox's jaw. The thief swore and fell back. The gun went flying, skittering under the rows of seats. Fox dived in the direction of the gun. Nick dived for the criminal, jumped on him, knocking him to the ground.

A handful of passengers were beginning to rise now, with that look that meant they were ready and willing to help just as soon as they best knew how. Oh, how he loved that look.

"Everybody stay back, and somebody find the gun!" Nick shouted.

A final lurch shook the car. Erica got to her feet and turned toward the front of the train. If the train was really separating, what would happen to the back half? Which part would her son be in when the train pulled away? And would she be left behind without him? There was no way she was about to let that happen. She'd been separated from her son for long enough.

She glanced back to where Nick was battling Fox on the floor now, thankful he was still wearing his fatigues.

"Listen to Corporal Nick Henry!" she shouted. "He's a soldier with the Canadian Rangers! He'll tell you what to do."

Heads swiveled in his direction. Nick looked up and it was only the fear of losing her son that enabled her to look away. She turned and ran, pushing through the double doors onto the gangway separating the passenger and dining car, just in time to see a large man with a dark beard charge out of the dining car toward her. It was Orson.

"Hands up!" he ordered.

No, not this time. She was done with cooperating. She was done with playing nice. And his weapon was still in his holster. He reached for his gun, but she was faster. She lowered her head, raised her elbows in front of her like a battering ram and barreled into him, knocking the air from his lungs before he even managed to get off a shot. He grunted and fell back, winded. The gun fell from his grasp. Real or replica, she didn't know. But either way she wasn't about to let him grab hold of it and she could use it to hit him. She snatched the weapon up and leveled a swift, hard strike to his face. Something cracked. He grabbed for his nose. Was there time to search him for more weapons? No. But she could get away faster than he could recover from having been pistol whipped.

Erica darted into the dining car and heard the door shut behind her as she pelted toward the end. She yanked the door open, expecting to see the first-class car, and instead almost tumbled into the two-foot gap between the cars. Rain coursed between the cars. The train had already separated. The front of the train was already pulling away. She braced herself to jump onto the front half of the train. *Goodbye, Nick.*

"Mommy!"

"Erica, stay there!"

Two voices came at once, filling her heart. Then she saw her brother running toward her through the first-class car, holding Zander in his arms. Fear filled her son's eyes. His tiny hands clasped his uncle's neck. Oh, Tommy. Her brother had grabbed her son and made a run for it. The gap between the cars grew.

Three feet.

"Step back!" Tommy yelled. "I'm going to jump!"

A shot rang out from the air behind him.

Four feet.

"Get down now!" Mr. Grand charged down the cabin. "So much as flinch, and I'll shoot."

Her brother groaned and dropped to his knees. Zander's arms reached out for her. "Mommy!"

Five feet.

She gritted her teeth. There was only one thing left to do. She flung the door into locked-open position, ran a few steps back, then turned and sprinted full tilt for the departing train. Her foot hit the edge. She leaped, throwing her body into the wind and rain, bracing herself to feel the relentless, hard tracks beneath her if she fell short and plummeted to the ground. *Lord, help me now!* Her shins smacked against the doorway of the departing rail car. The momentum of the train tossed her backward, threatening to throw her off again. Then she felt her brother's strong, rough and reassuring hand grab her jacket and yank her in. She collapsed onto the floor and gasped for breath.

"Hey, sis. You okay?"

"Thank you," she huffed. Finding two words was all her breath could muster.

Thank You, thank You, God.

"Mommy!" Zander squirmed away from her brother and dived into her arms.

"Hey, Little Soldier. It's so good to see you." She clutched him tightly. "You okay?"

He hid his head in her neck and nodded. "I was brave, Mama."

"I'm sure you were."

"Where's Soldier Nick?"

Tears choked in her throat. "Fighting the bad guys."

"Get up!" Mr. Grand's voice came from above her. The weapon in his hand was all too real. "It's about time you joined us."

The gun sat heavy in her pocket, along with the question of whether it was real or fake. Ei-

ther way, she expected that Mr. Grand or somebody on his crew would search her. But maybe
he wouldn't search her brother. Nick's warning about her brother filled her mind. But he
didn't know Tommy like she did. Yes, he'd always been loudmouthed and easily provoked,
with a tendency to fight first and think second
when offended. But there were only so many
jobs a man could lose and only so many estab-
lishments he could get kicked out of before he
started to learn some self-control. And right
now there was no one else left to trust.

She pivoted as she climbed to her feet, cradling her son with one arm. With the other hand
she slid the gun from her pocket and eased it
around the floor toward her brother, blocking
Mr. Grand's view with her son. For a fraction
of a second, she thought Tommy was going to
miss it and she felt her heart seize. Then she
sensed Tommy pulling the gun from her hand.
She stood and faced Mr. Grand. Zander's face
pressed into her neck as she held her son tightly
with both arms.

Mr. Grand aimed his gun directly between
her eyes. "Nice try," he said. "But tell your
brother to toss the gun or things are going to
get ugly."

Erica winced as she heard the gun she'd worked so hard at smuggling into her brother's hands clatter to the floor.

Now what, Lord?

Mr. Grand frowned. "Come with me. I have something to show you."

Erica looked at the man behind the weapon. "You look tired," she said, "and like you've lost control of the heist."

But the only response she got was the sound of him swearing under his breath. She allowed herself one quick glance at the back half of the train as it disappeared into the rain and darkness behind them.

"Goodbye, Nick," she whispered, feeling her heart yank her back to where she'd left him fighting for his life and the lives of the passengers around them. Was he still alive? Would she ever see him again? *I'm going to miss you so much. I'm so sorry I never properly introduced you to your son.*

Then she turned her head back and walked toward Mr. Grand, as the only man she'd ever loved became farther and farther behind her.

Nick was still down on the ground. Not quite the longest fist fight he'd ever been in, but the fact that Fox was twice his size and they were trapped in a cramped train aisle with civilians all around definitely complicated matters. Thanks to one final, decisive blow, he'd knocked Fox down. Nick pressed the criminal into the floor on his stomach. *Now, to get some answers.* Last time he hadn't been all that talkative. But pulling a gun in a crowded economy car was definitely an escalation; Nick had watched this man's boss both strand people and kill Clark, and the train had definitely stopped.

Not to mention Erica had taken off running.

"Tell me nobody's going to hurt the boy or his mother," Nick demanded. "Tell me he's going to be safe."

Fox rolled his jaw but didn't speak. Maybe one too many blows had left him even more winded than Nick felt. Or, more likely, Fox didn't know.

Nick looked around at a sea of widened passenger eyes watching him from every direction. Now to find out what had happened to Fox's gun and where Erica had gone.

"Do you know why the train has stopped?"

Fox cut his eyes to the ceiling. Yeah, that looked like a "Nope."

"Look, I don't want to fight you," Nick said,

feeling his voice drop, level and calm. "And I'm guessing fighting me wasn't in your plan. I think you agreed to do a job, it got out of hand and now you're caught up in something you can't control. I'm guessing that you and your buddies were hired to help Mr. Grand steal a case from a train. That's it. Hop the train, grab a case and everybody goes home happy. Job probably looked too easy.

"But then things kept changing on you and nothing turned out as planned. I'm also guessing this is your first job from Mr. Grand. Because I can't imagine a pro like you taking a second job from a man who's a mess like this. So let's stop exchanging punches and find a way out of this where nobody dies."

Yeah, this was who he was now. He was a corporal. He was an instructor. He was the kind of man who stopped fights instead of ran from them. And he was thankful to God that he was.

Fox's mouth spit out a string of vile invectives. His eyes said, *Yup*.

Nick pulled a red bandanna from his pocket and gagged Fox, just enough to mute the noise. This man wasn't a planning criminal. He was a hired gun, nothing more. And Nick still had a stopped train, a missing weapon and a frightened audience to worry about. Then, through the muffled fabric, Nick caught two words loud and clear: *train waitress*.

"She's a train attendant." Nick leaned in and pulled the bandanna out. "And what did you say about her?"

"You're worried about her, right?" Fox practically spit. "All this is her fault. She's the reason all this went down."

Nick's heart stuttered. "What do you mean? What's her fault? The fact the heist went off the rails? Or something else?"

No answer. *Okay, conversation over.* He retied the gag around the man's mouth and then sat back, fished his military service identification from his pocket and held it high.

"As Erica mentioned, my name is Nick Henry," he called out. "I'm from Huntsville, Ontario, and I'm a corporal with the Canadian Rangers stationed out of Petawawa. I'm incredibly sorry you all had to witness this. There has been an incident on the train, but I want to reassure you I'm doing everything in my power to keep everyone safe. Now, does anyone happen to have a satellite phone? Because, as you probably know, regular cell service isn't working."

He decided to omit the fact that they hadn't

managed to reach the authorities—along with the news of what had happened to Clark and the train staff—to de-escalate things the best he could for now. More eyes met his. That was good, people were listening. But still, the audience was mostly frozen, which, while normal in a shock situation, didn't make his life any easier now. He'd need somebody to help him deal with Fox, not to mention that he had to figure out what to do now that one of the thieves had pulled a weapon in front of everyone.

Several passengers had run out of the car and into the car behind them during the kerfuffle, and Nick had lost eyes on the man in the blazer he'd pegged as private security—he guessed he'd evacuated the suits he was accompanying and was maybe even helping some of the others. Which, if so, was great and probably him doing his job, but still. As for the elderly gentleman with military bearing, his tall form now seemed to be protectively cradling his wife, who was huddling under the seats. So Nick was on his own.

Nick plowed on. "Also, while I have your attention, has anybody seen a gun? A handgun. Specifically a Glock 17, about nine by nineteen inches, with a muzzle at one end and a trigger in the middle?"

The door crashed open behind him. Nick's head whipped around. Orson staggered through, looking like his face had just met the wrong end of a fight. His nose was crooked, swollen and bloody. His hand was waving a very small but nonetheless lethal handgun at nobody in particular.

"You! Soldier! Stand up and put your hands in the air!" Orson snapped. He stumbled forward so unsteadily that for a moment, if Nick didn't know any better, he'd think the train was still moving. "Somebody tell me. Where's… the…waitress who did this to me?"

Orson punctuated the gaps between words with some of the ugliest swear words and insults Nick had ever heard weaponized against a woman, and instinctively he felt his ears edit them out.

The waitress? Erica? Hang on. Was he saying that Erica was the one who'd broken his nose? Pride surged through Nick. So Zander was right—whatever she'd hit Orson with, it seemed Erica could pack quite the wallop.

Nobody answered. Orson staggered forward and aimed his gun at Nick.

"You! Soldier! Get off him, get down on the floor and put your hands behind your head. Or I'm going to start shooting people, got it?" He swung the gun toward the elderly couple. The old woman was still cowering and now she seemed to be shaking. "One by one, until we got bodies littering the floor. Got it?"

"Loud and clear." Nick gritted his teeth and rose slowly, feeling Fox slide out from under him and hating the fact he was letting the criminal go. Fox yanked the gag from his mouth, grabbed Nick by the back of the neck and shoved him down hard.

So now he was trapped in a train car, on a stranded train, in the middle of the night and in the middle of nowhere, with a smattering of passengers, one criminal to his back and another in front of him. The thieves exchanged a look. If Nick had to guess what was happening, Mr. Grand's plan was spinning even further off course and these two thugs, tired of being told what to do, had decided to go freelance. Seemed there truly was no honor among thieves. But if it was every crook for himself, Nick doubted that would make them any safer.

Okay, God, how exactly am I going to get

*out of this one? There's only so much I can do
alone. Please, God. I need some help right now.*

"Everyone!" Orson barked. "This is a hijacking! You're all going to get out your bags
and open them. We want wallets, jewelry, wedding rings, phones, laptops, electronics, knives,
credit cards, debit cards, ID's—everything and
anything you've got. Okay? Everything. And if
you hide something from us, we'll know.

"My buddy Fox is going to grab a bag and
we're going to start collecting. Then when I
say the word, you're all going to walk single
file into the next car, with your hands on your
heads. You're going to do exactly what you're
told or I'm going to kill each and every one of
you."

The gunshot cracked the air so suddenly
Nick didn't know where it had come from and
so unexpectedly his brain couldn't begin to process. Thankfully, his instincts had always been
good at kicking in and letting his brain catch
up later. The bullet caught Orson in the arm.
He howled in pain as his body snapped back.
Nick sprang onto his heels, swung his elbow
back and tossed Fox off him. Only then did he
look back to see where the shot had come from.

Nick's jaw dropped. The elderly man's tiny

gray-haired wife stood behind them, smoke still swirling from the muzzle of the gun she held in both hands with clear military precision. Well, guess that answered the question of where the gun had gone and why she'd been under the seats.

"Corporal!" The woman's sharp blue eyes cut in his direction as her voice rose with a ring of authority that had every molecule in his body springing to attention. "Secure the hostile at the front of the car. Secure his weapon. We'll cover this one."

That was all Nick needed to hear. He charged down the narrow aisle between the seats like a linebacker and lunged for Orson, throwing him back against the wall and taking him to the ground. Orson flailed wildly, reaching for his gun, blood seeping through his jacket from the bullet wound in his shoulder. Nick didn't give him the chance. Instead he yanked Orson back, pressed him to the floor and pinned him hard.

He glanced back. Two passengers were re-straining Fox at the elderly woman's direction.

"I need a belt or some rope," he shouted. "Something I can tie his hands with!"

Within a second, two belts and a bungee cord had landed beside him from various corners

of the car. They were followed by the smattering sounds of nervous clapping and laughing.
Okay, good. Passengers were starting to un-
freeze. He let himself smile, grabbed the cord,
flipped Orson over and bound his hands hard.
He flipped him back over and propped him up
against the wall in a seated position.

Orson glared at him and swore. His face
looked even worse up close.

"Did Erica, the red-haired train attendant,
really break your nose?" Nick asked, knowing the truth even before he saw the confirmation flicker in the thief's eyes and heard the
words spew from his mouth. And while, as a
Canadian soldier and peacekeeper, Nick had a
deeply rooted belief that violence should always
be the last possible resort in a conflict situation, his heart was flooded with both relief and
pride that the tenacious girl he'd once fallen for
had grown up to be someone so strong, brave
and capable of defending herself. No man in
his right mind would have ever let a woman
like her go. "Where is she? Where did she go?
Is she okay? How is her son?"

No answers. Just more threats and swearing.
Fortunately, Nick had another bandanna handy
to gag this one, as well.

"Corporal?" The woman's voice rang with authority and snapped his attention back. "Everything secure?"

"Yes, ma'am." He got to his feet and turned back. The diminutive gray-haired woman had passed the weapon to her stately husband. Fox lay on the floor, bound and gagged again, restrained by two passengers. The elderly couple exchanged a look that didn't just speak volumes but entire libraries. And suddenly Nick found himself both thinking of his own parents and wondering if he'd ever have that kind of connection with someone. He paused for a moment, waiting for the couple to introduce themselves and not sure how to ask them who they were. Then he went for the simplest solution.

"I'm Corporal Nick Henry, 4th Canadian Division Support Base, Petawawa."

"Warrant Officer Dorothy Collins," she replied. "Retired, of the Loyal Edmonton Regiment, 4th Battalion, Princess Patricia's Canadian Light Infantry." So she'd seen serious combat, he imagined, in both Korea and Afghanistan. She glanced at her husband.

"Colonel William Collins," he said. "Retired, of the King's Own Calgary Regiment."

The elderly man's voice was softer and frailer than his wife's, but his bearing showed every bit the rank he'd earned. *Talk about a power couple.* William outranked Dorothy, but she'd probably seen more first-line combat. Nick fought the urge to whistle and saluted instead.

"Sorry for leaving you hanging as long as we did, Corporal," William added. "But Dorothy felt it important to check the weapon thoroughly, to make sure it was loaded, before engaging." *So that's what she'd been doing under the seat.* Something twinkled in William's eyes. "She's always been the better shot."

"What are we looking at?" Dorothy asked. "Are there more hostiles on the train?"

"Four more hostiles that I know of," Nick said. "At least two, maybe three, hostages in the front of the train, including a child. One fatality—a passenger. Again, that I know of. It's an apparent theft situation. They pressed a train attendant into helping them steal a case from the baggage compartment and ordered the rest of the crew off when we stopped briefly. I don't know who's driving the train or why it's not stopped.

"I know these two men only as Orson and Fox. Until a few moments ago, my understanding was that this was a simple, small-scale theft—specifically for a laptop that belonged to the North Jewels Diamond Mine—and they weren't planning on initiating a large-scale hostage situation." Now things were quickly becoming anything but simple. "Internet and outside phone lines are down. I think our priorities should be securing the hostiles in the baggage compartment, making sure the passengers are safe and separated from the hostiles, and establishing contact with the outside world. Also, the fatality is Member of Provincial Parliament Clark Lemain."

A gasp of recognition moved through the car. Again, the couple exchanged a look.

Nick took a deep breath. "My main concern right now is locating my..." His voice trailed off. Former best friend? Ex-girlfriend? Biggest regret? "The train attendant I was with... She ran to the front of the train when it stopped. Her son was taken hostage."

Did the desperation and fear he felt show in the tone of his voice? William and Dorothy now exchanged a longer, more pointed look, and for a moment he was afraid the two retired officers, who clearly outranked him, were going to insist that he stay to help secure the train.

"Please," he said. "She knows the train better than anyone. She knows the front engineer, who we suspect might also be a hostage and is being forced or coerced into driving the train. If we have any hope of restoring power to the affected systems and communication with the outside world, and securing the train, we need her."

He heard the strain in his voice. *I need her. In a way I can't even explain.*

"Go." Dorothy nodded. "We'll secure the passengers. Don't take any unnecessary risks."

"Thank you, ma'am. I'll be back as soon as I can."

Hopefully with Erica by his side, Zander in his arms and the irrefutable knowledge that the crisis had ended and help was on its way. *It's what I'm hoping for, praying for and going to do whatever it takes to make happen.*

He turned and sprinted out of the car, through the gangway and into the dining car. It was deserted. He kept running. Silence filled the train ahead. No, more than silence. A darkness and emptiness that seemed to loom larger with every step. Were the lights off? Had something happened to the front of the train? No. No, it couldn't be. He reached the door, yanked it open and stood there, heartache wringing pain from his lungs with every breath. Empty tracks spread ahead of his eyes. Wind and rain lashed against his body. He peered into the darkness, hoping to see even the faintest flicker of light emanating from the tracks ahead of him. But it was useless.

The cars had detached. The front of the train was gone. The rear of the train had been left behind. He'd been left behind. Without Erica.

No, Lord! No! He stumbled back from the doorway, his legs feeling so weak he almost fell to his knees. This couldn't be happening. She couldn't be gone. Erica couldn't be gone.

Suddenly his knees locked straight as he felt the unmistakable jab of a revolver in the small of his back.

"Hey, buddy, stand up." The male voice in his ear was rough, deep and somehow perfectly matched the strength of the grip of the hand now grabbing his shoulder. "I got somebody on the phone who wants to talk to you."

SEVEN

Nick suddenly tensed to spin and fight while his eyes stared out ahead at the empty tracks where Erica had gone. The gun pressed deeper into his back.

"Who are you?" he asked.

The man chuckled. It was a sound that somehow made him think of a body of water that was so deep it was hard to reach the bottom.

"Liam Bearsmith," he said slowly, as if he expected his name would mean something to Nick for some reason. It didn't. "I'm an economic real estate consultant who procures hard-to-obtain properties for elite clientele." Not a word of which Nick believed. "This conversation never happened."

Okay, that he believed. "You got it, buddy."

"Have you heard of me?" he asked. "Do you know who I am?"

"Nope," Nick said. "Not a clue. Should I?"

Liam Bearsmith sighed and didn't answer Nick's question. He eased his grip. "I suggest you turn around and close the door behind you, Corporal Nick Henry, before you fall out the train onto the tracks."

Nick turned around slowly and slid the door shut behind him.

The man in the dark blazer, whom he'd pegged as private security, had a meticulous Smith & Wesson semiautomatic in his left hand. Something that would've been handy for Nick to have had earlier in this adventure.

Liam Bearsmith glanced past him. One eyebrow rose. "Huh, well that's something I did not expect. Do you happen to have any idea where the front of the train went?"

"Your guess is as good as mine," Nick said. Despite the gun pointed at him, Nick felt the urge to cross his arms. "I'm guessing your boss, Mr. Grand, decided to leave us here and take it somewhere."

Now both eyebrows rose.

"First off, I have no idea who Mr. Grand is," Liam said. The grit deepened in his voice and Nick had the distinct impression of fire burning under the rocks. "I am not working for him.

And whatever amateur-hour heist this is that we've somehow stumbled into, it's definitely not something I wanted to see happen today. I'm just a kindly real estate consultant who unfortunately chose the wrong train."

Nick snorted.

Liam ignored it. "I'm sorry for the gun, but in my experience people tend to be a bit unpredictable when they're having a bad day. And yours appears to be a doozy." His left hand reached into his pocket and Nick instinctively stepped back to strike.

"Whoa, buddy," Liam said. "I'm just the middle man. Somebody wants to talk to you."

His other hand rose and Nick suddenly realized what he was holding. It was a satellite phone.

"So, you had a gun and a satellite phone, and did nothing while a woman was kidnapped and a soldier was threatened at gunpoint?" Nick forced the words through clenched teeth.

Yeah, it probably was a good idea that Mr. Liam Bearsmith—whoever he was—had decided to show up armed. Otherwise, Nick might not have overcome the impulse to clock him.

"Don't be an idiot," Liam snapped. "I noticed your friend being held at gunpoint and intervened the best I could under the particular circumstances I was in."

Nick blinked.

"You tripped her."

"I verbally intervened," Liam said with a tone that left no doubt which one of them was still holding a weapon. "And I physically separated her from the man holding her. Then you stepped in and apparently had it covered, so I switched my attention to evacuating as many people as I could from the vicinity. You have no idea what I'm jeopardizing and risking by even talking to you. Now, tell me who you are again."

"Corporal Nick Henry. But you already knew that. Now, who are you and what are you playing at?"

The man's steely glare told him nothing. "From?"

"Fourth Canadian Division Support Base—"

"Before that?"

"Huntsville, Ontario. What does this—"

"Trust me, buddy, I like this even less than you do. But I owe somebody my life and this is the best way I know to repay it. Last question—what's your sister's name?"

"My sister?" The words stopped Nick's breath.

A sudden, inexplicable cold swept over him, choking his lungs. He felt an old, reflexive smile turn on his face. It was the forced smile of the joker he'd once been. It was the smile of a man who didn't talk about things he didn't want to talk about and skated circles over the thin ice of conversations he didn't want to have without ever looking down at just how thin the ice was he was skating on. "I don't have a sister. I have three older brothers. Max is a paramedic. Trent and Jacob are cops—"

"This isn't a game," Liam snapped. "And you're wasting time. You care about that Erica chick and her kid? Tell me you sister's name!"

"Faith." The single word caught in his throat like someone was yanking it out from somewhere deep inside him. "She was murdered, at the age of twelve, by a man who'd been trying to abduct her, probably a serial killer, before I was born."

It was the reason his family had been broken. It was the reason he was damaged. It was the reason he'd self-destructed and hurt the only woman he'd ever loved.

Liam sighed. Humanity, pain and something almost like compassion washed over the man's face. "I'm sorry for your loss," he said, and there was a depth to the words that was almost like Nick was hearing them for the first time.

Liam pushed a button on the phone. "Yeah, it's him," he told whoever was on the other end. "You could've warned me what a stubborn pain he was. This never happened. Tell your lovely fiancée we're now even."

He stretched his arm out. "It's for you."

So Nick had gathered. He took the phone. "Hello?"

"Yo, bro!" Trent's voice floated down the line, filled the phone, as comforting and strong as if his older brother was there, in person, standing beside him. "How's it going?"

"Trent?" Gratitude washed over Nick. He glanced at Liam Bearsmith, who was suddenly very preoccupied with checking out a random spot on the ceiling. "I... It's... Hi... I have literally never been this happy to hear your voice before."

Trent chuckled. For years he had been undercover with the RCMP Vice Unit, working to take down some of the worst gangs in Canada, until one life-threatening assignment, with his now fiancée, Detective Chloe Brant, had changed everything. Did that mean Liam Bearsmith was also an undercover detective on a long-term assignment? That would explain why he'd been cautious about blowing his cover and leaping into action. And why he'd wondered if Nick had heard of him. Was he in Vice like Trent? Or…? No. Something about the pity and sympathy, and even the empathy that had flooded his eyes when he'd mentioned Nick's sister made him suspect Liam was with a Special Victims Unit like Chloe. He shuddered to think of what kind of operation the man was working on.

A thousand questions leaped into Nick's mind like popcorn overflowing the pot. He didn't know which to ask first. An unexpected one slipped out. "How does an undercover cop know about Faith? Does this mean people are still investigating her death? That the case hasn't been dropped? That there's still hope of catching whoever killed her?"

"Nick." Trent's voice was surprisingly gentle. "Liam Bearsmith is a real estate consultant for elite clients. He's a good and very reliable man who's known Chloe for many years and takes on very long-term projects that other real estate agents won't go anywhere near. You need to pretend you've never met him and promptly forget everything you know about him. This is a secure line. This conversation never happened, and you know better than to ask me questions about things I can't answer."

But if it involves our sister...

"Now," Trent said, "tell me what's going on."

Nick swallowed hard, rolled his shoulders back and quickly gave Trent a situation report, leaving out everything personal and just highlighting the facts. He could almost hear his brother nodding, focusing on the current situation and not the situation that had got them there. He suspected Liam had already briefed him on as much as he knew.

"The lack of roads is definitely going to be an evacuation challenge," Trent said. "And the storm isn't great for air rescue. No pilot in their right mind would fly in weather like this. But we'll get one team to find and rescue the stranded crew, another to meet the rear portion of the train and a third to intersect the front part of the train before it reaches Moosonee."

Nick glanced at his watch. It was nearing one in the morning. It had been almost two hours since the crisis had started and law enforcement was only hearing about it now. Who knew how long it would take for a rescue crew to start arriving?

"There are only two known hostiles in the rear part of the train and they've been subdued," Nick added. "We've got electricity, power and water. We should be fine to wait for rescue. But it's the front part of the train I'm worried about. I need to get to them somehow. The stolen laptop was from North Jewels Diamond Mine. The woman who checked it in the baggage cart was ordered off the train at gunpoint and then stranded with the crew. Your RCMP division investigated North Jewels for funneling diamonds to organized crime. Is there anything you can tell me?"

"Not without breaking a few laws," Trent said. "Although we can't discount the possibility somebody linked to organized crime set up the heist or that this is somehow an attempt to interfere with the investigation. Also, maybe coincidentally, Clark Lemain was one of a handful of politicians claiming the RCMP overstretched its reach and that the charges are baseless."

"And now Clark is dead." Nick huffed out a long breath. "I can't imagine how that's going to impact the country. Even people who didn't like him knew who he was. It's probably because I grew up around you and Jacob, but I wondered if his murder could've been a targeted hit. He was the only person besides the criminals to book a first-class sleeper cabin. But I'm sure there are easier ways to assassinate a politician than hijacking a train."

"There was also talk that some of his former campaign staffers were going to go to the police about him, over something," Trent said. "I don't know the details. Rumor was harassment."

A long pause filled the phone. Nick knew he needed to tell Trent about Erica. But he didn't know how.

"Bearsmith said you were in a near panic about a woman and child," Trent said. "That's why he broke protocol and contacted me. Is she someone you know?"

"We know," Nick said. "It's Erica Knight. She has a son, a little boy named Zander. Her brother Tommy's with them, too."

He heard his brother whisper a prayer under his breath.

"Okay," Trent said. "We've already got a rescue team scrambling. It's a joint RCMP, OPP and military operation. Help is on its way, bro. It's going to be okay."

Help was on its way to three separate, hard-to-reach locations, in the northern Ontario wilderness, in the dark and in a rainstorm.

"I need to find a way to get to the front of the train," Nick said. "I can't leave Erica and Zander there alone."

"I know how you feel," Trent said. Nick closed his eyes and could almost feel his brother's hand on his shoulder. "But you've got to stay put. Okay? There's nothing you can do."

"How can I stay put?"

"Because you have to," Trent said. "Because there's nothing you can do. I have unlimited faith in you. You know I do. But you're not about to single-handedly stop a train hijacking. So, please, promise me you'll stay put. I've got to hang up now. But it's going to be okay. I promise. I love ya, bro."

"You, too." Nick sighed. "Tell Jacob and Max I might be a bit late meeting them for breakfast in Moosonee tomorrow."

"Will do."

Nick ended the call and turned around. Liam Bearsmith was looking at him. Nick wondered how much he'd heard.

"I've got to go after them," Nick said. "I can't just leave them alone in the train."

The man, who was most certainly a detective and probably not named Liam, nodded.

"I got a really sweet motorcycle in the baggage car," he said. "I expect I'm going to have to report it stolen."

Erica sat cross-legged on the floor of the first-class car lounge, with her son playing soldier beside her in a tent she'd helped him rig by suspending a small lounge blanket between two sleeper chairs. Mr. Grand had let her son keep his plastic toys, which Zander was now quietly marching around inside. She thanked God for whatever it was inside little children that pushed their minds to play and distract themselves even in the worst situations. The phrase "Thank God for small mercies" had never felt truer.

She didn't know if Mr. Grand had some softness or personal code when it came to children or if whoever had hired him had told him not to hurt kids. But she'd barely been on the front half of the train for a few minutes when Mr. Grand had tossed a blanket at her and told her to cover her son's face and shield his eyes. She had, cradling Zander to her chest and cover-

ing him in the blanket like she used to when
he was a tiny baby and she'd rock him to sleep.

Then any tiny sliver of hope Erica had had
that Clark wasn't actually dead withered and
died as she watched Lou half drag, half carry
a bloody body in a blue suit, with a large head
wound, through the first-class lounge and toss
it out the back door onto the tracks. Her heart
was too horrified to beat. Dizziness had swept
over her, worse than any morning sickness had
ever been.

He could've disposed of Clark's body at any
time. But instead Mr. Grand had made sure
she'd seen. He'd wanted her to see. He'd wanted
to make her see it was her fault a man she'd
known and grown up with was dead.

Since then she hadn't been able to get that
image and knowledge out of her mind.

*Lord, have mercy. Be with Clark's family,
his friends, his constituents and everyone he
loved. Please, get everyone else out of this alive
and unharmed.*

Who would do all this for a laptop? What
could ever be on that laptop—even one belong-
ing to a diamond mine—that would be worth
killing for?

Now the two-car-long train continued its

journey north through the night. Zander played in his tent. Erica's brother sat on the floor opposite her. Although their kidnappers had left her and Zander free to roam the small space, Lou had tied Tommy's legs together, probably to keep him from running again. But so far he'd left Tommy's hands free. She guessed so he could help her with Zander.

Tommy's head was bowed as if trying to get any sleep he could. How had he not managed to hide the gun? Considering all the stuff her brother had smuggled in and out of the house past their mother, how had he managed to let Mr. Grand see the gun? She sighed and reminded herself that his friend was dead and she couldn't imagine what he'd been going through keeping her son safe.

To her right, the blond-haired young woman named Julie sat at the stolen laptop, her fingers typing furiously, while Mr. Grand stood over her. To her left, Lou stood over them, periodically and lazily waving his semiautomatic in their direction. She didn't see the young, gangly Rowan anywhere and wondered if he'd been assigned the job of keeping his weapon trained on Bob, to make sure the engineer did as he was told. Or if something worse had happened to Rowan.

Bob, what did they do to get you to do this? Did they threaten you? Hurt you? Pay and bribe you? If only she could get to him, maybe she could get him to stop the train.

Erica stretched, thankful her hands and feet hadn't been bound. Had they only bound Tommy's legs because they thought he was a threat and she wasn't? It was not like there was much she could do against a crew of people with weapons. It was not like they had the ability to overpower them and take the train. Or like she was about to risk her and Zander's lives by jumping out of the train in the middle of nowhere.

No. For now all she could do was sit on the floor, letting the unspoken threat of the gun-wielding thug on the door and the vulnerability of the precious child playing quietly beside her keep her rooted in place, while her mind took in all the information it could as she prayed and waited for when she could make her move.

My family and I are not going to die here, Lord. Not like this. Please, let me know when to act. Let me know what to do.

At least she now had far more information

than she had about what was going on. The fact Mr. Grand kept popping periodically into the front engine and one of the sleeper cabins made her suspect he had a satellite phone or some other way to contact the outside world and was still in touch with either an accomplice or whoever had hired him. From the snippets of hushed conversation Erica had been able to overhear, it seemed Mr. Grand wanted Julie to find and download the contents of the laptop before he handed it over to his client. It also seemed like she wasn't having any success.

Zander slipped out of his tent and went over to the window and looked out. His small figures danced along the ledge. She held her breath a moment, but nobody stopped him. *Thank You, God. If Zander's safety had depended on him sitting still, I don't know what I'd do.*

She glanced at her brother. Tommy inched his body closer.

"You okay?" she whispered.

Tommy nodded. "Yeah. Zander's been great, and they've treated us well. But…" His voice trailed off as pain filled his eyes.

"Clark…" she finished, then shot a glance toward Zander. "I'm so sorry."

Tommy closed his eyes and nodded. "I keep asking why him and not me."

"Me, too." She reached into the gap between them for her brother's hand. He squeezed it. Then she pulled back. "How did you get away?"

"There was some kind of panic in the front engine," Tommy said. "The engineer needed help detaching the train. Everyone was distracted. Mr. Grand and Lou ran off. They left me alone with Julie and Rowan. I didn't think they'd shoot me—I just had a hunch they might not. So I seized the moment, scooped up Zander and ran. I'm just sorry I didn't get farther."

"It's okay," she said. "You did more than enough."

He nodded but she wasn't sure he believed her.

"Where's Rowan now?" she asked.

Tommy shrugged. "No idea. Front engine, I think."

"I told Uncle Tommy about the soldier, Mommy," Zander told her as he turned from the window. "And how he helped us."

Tommy nodded. "He sounds like a good guy."

He's more than a good guy. He's Nick. My Nick. And you never told him I was pregnant.

And yeah, maybe you had your reasons, but now I'm worried that I'm never going to see him again and he's never going to know that he has a son.

Words tumbled through her mind, but for now she'd keep them to herself. She'd tell Tommy that Nick had been the one to save them after this was all done. For now, she didn't need that argument. She'd tell Nick the truth, too. Soon. She had to grab the hope of that and hold it tightly.

Zander's attention turned back to the window. The finger tapping grew faster.

Mr. Grand leaned over Julie's shoulder and barked something. Then he grabbed her by the shoulder. His voice rose. Whatever he thought was on that laptop, he wanted Julie to find it faster.

Erica nodded in their direction. "Any idea what that's all about?"

"Clark had been going on for weeks about this whole idea that the North Jewels Diamond Mine investigation was corrupt from the start," Tommy said. "He just found the whole idea that a mine was funneling diamonds to organized crime to be preposterous. And when he found out that the guy who headed the investigation—

Trent Henry—was the older brother of your idiot ex-boyfriend, Nick, that settled it for him. He started digging until he found something."

Clark had dug up evidence that Nick's brother had botched a major investigation? That didn't seem likely. "What did he find?"

"Offshore bank accounts with large amounts of money in them. Proof that diamonds had instead been sold to some overseas buyers. All the proof—bank account numbers, trace numbers, smuggling routes—are all supposedly on that laptop."

Well, at least that would explain why someone would steal the laptop and why Mr. Grand was in such a hurry to copy the data. There was no limit to what an enterprising criminal could do with information like that.

"Then who brought the laptop on the train?"

"Apparently, a whistle-blower." Tommy shrugged. "Clark said she contacted him. The mine is very isolated, and all electronic communications are monitored. The information was too sensitive to be sent electronically. So she smuggled it out on a laptop. Apparently, the plan was that Clark would then get it from the baggage compartment at Moosonee."

Only she didn't get off in Moosonee. She'd

been ordered out of the train in the middle of nowhere with the crew.

"But how was that even supposed to work?" Erica asked. "Only the person who checked the case in to the cabinet can check it out again..."

But the words trailed off her tongue even as she spoke them. *She* was the person responsible for enforcing that rule. She was the person Clark would've asked to take the case out of the cabinet for him. Had Clark set this whole thing up counting on the fact that he'd be able to sweet-talk Erica into breaking that rule for him? Was that why he'd invited her son and brother along for this trip? To distract her or somehow help convince her that he was a nice guy and she should do this favor for him?

"Tell me you didn't know about any of this before you got on the train with Zander," Erica said. "Please, tell me you didn't let Clark talk you into something stupid and put my son in danger."

His face paled, and the look of guilt that crossed it was one that she knew all too well and told her everything she needed to know.

"Oh, Tommy." A sickening feeling filled her heart. "What did you do?"

"I'm so sorry." Tommy's eyes begged her for

forgiveness. "Clark was nervous and wanted someone with him who he trusted to have his back! He said bringing Zander would make it look more natural."

Instinctively her hand rose and it took more self-control than she realized she had to lower it again instead of decking him.

"You gave them leverage over me!" Her whispered voice grew louder. "You gave them a way to use the most important thing in my life to threaten and force me to do what they wanted me to do!"

"I had no idea about Mr. Grand," Tommy said. "Or the hijacking or any of it. Neither did Clark! You've gotta know I'd never do anything to hurt Zander. I'd give my life for that kid!"

"Enough talking!" Mr. Grand waved the gun in their direction. "Both of you. Or I'll tie you up and gag your mouths. Is that what you want?"

No. Erica shook her head, pressed her lips together and dropped her gaze. Anger burned inside her, spreading like a determined fire through her veins. Of all the stupid things her brother had done, this was by far the worst. But she couldn't let emotion take over. She needed to focus. She had to find a way out of here. But her mind spun. It seemed like every answer she got opened up new questions. In life she'd always been drawn to a scientific and philosophical rule called Occam's razor that stated the simplest solution was usually the right one. Or as she used to joke to Nick when trying to help him cram for an exam or finish whatever last-minute homework assignment he'd forgotten to do: *KISH—Keep. It. Simple. Henry.*

There was nothing at all simple about this. Sure, Clark had always had a flare for the dramatic and maybe the whistle-blower had had good reasons for agreeing to do the drop-off that way. But it was all too cloak-and-dagger. It was all too complicated. Why use a train to do the handoff? Why risk not being able to get the case from the secure storage cabinet? Had the story Clark told Tommy even been true?

No, there had to be something else going on. *What am I missing, Lord? What can I not see?*

Nick's unbidden face filled her mind. The way his lips had felt brushing over hers. The way his hand had felt when their fingers linked. The curve of his arm when she'd lain against him. His arms around her.

The stirring in her core when their eyes

had first met had been like a tremor shaking the walls of her heart that had grown stronger with each passing moment they'd been together. Being next to him had been like a dream she'd never let herself have. She liked him. She cared about him. She missed him. She'd… She'd never fully closed the part of her heart that he'd opened.

"Mommy! Look! There's something coming!" Zander called out.

Erica looked up, feeling her brain switch in an instant from the lovelorn girl she'd once been to the woman she was now.

He banged his palms on the window. "Come see!"

"Get down!" Mr. Grand shouted. He waved his gun at the little boy, whose nose was now pressed up against the windowpane. But it was like her son was so fixated on what he could see outside that he didn't even hear him. Zander got like that whenever he was excited about something.

Mr. Grand's voice rose. "I said get down!"

"It's okay. It's okay. Let me!" Erica sprang to her feet. The last thing she needed was Zander's tendency to get hyperfocused on things to put his life in danger now. Her hand brushed his back. "Zander, honey. Come on. We gotta sit down."

"No! Can't!" His head shook. A wide, excited smile spread across his face that belied everything about the situation they were in right now and she didn't know whether to be thankful or worried. Probably both. "Look! Someone's coming!"

"No, honey, I'm sorry." The words flew from her mouth automatically and sadly as her hand brushed his back. "Nobody's—"

But even as she spoke she felt the words freeze on her lips. There was a light. A single bright light shining behind them in the darkness. Her heart leaped. What was it? What was she seeing? She didn't know. All she knew was that something was cutting through the storm and shining in the darkness, and it was coming toward them. And suddenly she felt an unsettling fear creep up her spine. What if Zander was right, that this was a rescue and they'd just alerted the criminals to the fact that it was coming?

"Come on, Zander." She slid her arm around his waist. "Let's get down. Let's get away from the window." She scooped him up, spun him around and pushed him into Tommy's arms. Zander squirmed. His uncle held him tight.

"But, Mommy! What if it's Soldier Nick? What if he's coming to help us?"

Mr. Grand's head snapped up. He signaled Lou. "Go. Take care of it."

Lou nodded and disappeared down the first-class cabin. *No... Lord, please...* Then Mr. Grand yanked her by the arm and spun her around. He put one hand on her shoulder. With the other he pressed a gun into her ribs. "Come on. You're with me. If anyone tries anything funny, you're getting shot."

She glanced back at Tommy and then at Zander, thankful that Mr. Grand had positioned the weapon in such a way the little boy wouldn't see it. "I'll be right back. Don't worry. You be good for your uncle."

"It's the soldier, Mommy!" Zander's eyes grew wide and filled with hope. "It has to be!"

She didn't know whether to hope her son was right or to worry that he could be.

Mr. Grand walked her through the train car. Lou had shoved the back door open. The light came closer. She watched, fear mounting inside her. A man on a motorcycle drew closer. Lou leaned out the back door and fired. The motorcycle wove and dodged around trees and rocks, through the rain, evading the bullets flying toward him as he edged closer and closer to the train. And even with a helmet on, she knew every line of his form, his shoulders, his arms...

It was Nick.

Zander was right. The soldier, his daddy, the only man she'd ever loved and ever lost was coming toward them in the darkness.

"Shoot him!" Mr. Grand bellowed. "You can't let him reach the train!"

Lou fired again. Nick returned fire, his bullets striking so close to the back of the train that she thought for a moment he might actually take Lou down before the thug's bullet could reach him. Then suddenly Nick stopped firing. The gun paused in Nick's hand. As she watched, one of Lou's bullets hit its mark, a spark seeming to strike the motorcycle in the darkness. The bike flipped end over end.

"Nick! No!"

He was thrown like a rag doll from the motorcycle as it crashed in the darkness.

EIGHT

Nick's eyes closed and prayers crossed his heart as he felt his body fly helplessly through the air. He wasn't even sure what had happened. He'd actually thought he'd had it for a moment. He'd honestly thought he'd be able to catch up with the train, take out the thugs and somehow force it to stop. Instead he'd felt the motorcycle being yanked out from under him as suddenly and violently as if a grenade had gone off beneath him.

One image seared like a photo across the darkness of his mind.

Erica.

He'd seen Erica, standing there, framed by the doorway like a picture in a cameo or a locket, her flaming red hair highlighted by the light of the train surrounding her. She'd been standing behind the criminal who was firing at him. That had been his downfall. He'd realized two things at once. One was that if he fired and missed, or the bullet ricocheted, she could be hurt or worse. The other was that somehow he'd be okay if her face was the last thing his eyes ever saw.

Lord, please get me out of this alive...

His body curled, instinctively and protectively, thankful for the limited protection his fatigues and Liam Bearsmith's helmet and gloves gave him. Then he felt the impact of rock and earth smacking his body. His head snapped against the train tracks. The sound of the helmet cracking sounded like a whip in his ears. He lay there for a moment, pain radiating through his body. Then there was nothing but the rain beating down against him and the sound of the train pulling away, taking Erica and Zander with it.

He groaned, crawled onto his knees and yanked his helmet off. He let the cold rain beat against his head, run down his face and wash the hot tears of frustration from his eyes. He dropped to his knees. A deep anguish that eclipsed any pain his body was feeling moved through his core as a prayer for help ripped from his mouth as he cried out to God.

Erica and her son were gone. They'd been taken. Kidnapped. Stolen. Ripped away by killers. And he'd failed to save them. Now what? He couldn't chase after Erica and Zander on foot. And the walk back to the other half of the train would be long and painful. What other option did he have but to admit defeat? He dragged himself to his feet. The fact that he'd failed her weighed down on him like the X-ray vest he'd found himself under as a kid when he'd broken both a leg and a wrist after a spectacular wipeout on his brother Jacob's bike.

He'd failed her. He'd failed Erica Knight.

Out of every single person on the planet he could've completely and utterly failed to save, Erica was the one who could've ever hurt him the most.

He clenched his jaw and tried to block her sparkling dark eyes and dazzling smile from his mind, and almost succeeded. No, he'd gone six years without letting his mind get all tangled up in thoughts of her. He wasn't about to let himself fall all the way down the Erica hole in his mind now.

He felt around in his pocket for a small flashlight and swung the beam up and down the wet and empty tracks. The flashlight was one of the few items he'd managed to acquire with Liam's help after making sure the rear half of the train was secure, the passengers were safe and rescue was on its way. Along with his gun, which he'd lost somewhere in the darkness, he also had a knife, a lighter, emergency flares and a very nice radio walkie-talkie, which right now was picking up nothing but static on every channel. Sadly, no phone. High-tech satellite phones capable of operating where there was no cell service were pretty expensive and very rare, and the only one that had turned up had been Liam's. It made way more sense to leave the only phone capable of communicating with the outside world on a trainful of civilians than for Nick to take it on his solo mission. Not that he'd have been able to talk Liam into giving it to him anyway.

Well, no matter how helpless I feel, Lord, there are always things I can thank You for. So, thank You, God, that I'm alive. And that I got confirmation Erica is alive and well, too. Thank You that Liam Bearsmith was there and able to help Dorothy and William take care of the passengers in the back of the train. Please, be with all of them, keep them safe and help rescue reach them soon.

154 Rescuing His Secret Child

He found the motorcycle in a twisted wreck of metal a few feet away from where he remembered flipping. Looked like the thug had managed to shoot out the front tire, which would've been an impressive feat if Nick hadn't suspected the man had actually been aiming for his head. The bike was unsalvageable. There really was nothing left to do but walk. So he squared his shoulders, turned his back on the direction the departed train had gone and started for the front half of the train, wondering if rescue would reach them before he got there. He suspected not. Finding and reaching a train in the middle of nowhere, in the storm, was no easy feat.

Hopefully, whatever police or intelligence agency the man who called himself Liam Bearsmith worked for would replace his motorcycle. The bike had been a beautiful piece of machinery and Liam had looked almost pained as he'd helped Nick walk it out of the baggage car. He didn't envy the man trying to help maintain order and safety on the stranded train while also trying to maintain his undercover identity and not jeopardize whatever mission he was on. He prayed that God would protect Liam's undercover assignment, and also hoped that one day he'd find out more about the man and what kind of assignment he was working on.

Nick kept walking and found himself thinking about his brother Trent, who'd been so many different people and played so many different roles in his work as an undercover detective. Trent had been the first of the Henry brothers to find true love, proposing to fellow detective Chloe Brant, pretty much in the same moment he'd admitted he loved her. The wedding still hadn't happened, though. They'd opted for a long engagement, he suspected to give the two strong-willed, independent people time to get used to being partners in life and in love. Then Max had met Daisy, a nanny on the run for her life with a baby in her arms. That had been love at first sight and, a few weeks later, Max and Daisy had been married in a small, casual ceremony at the Henry family farmhouse, with her son, Fitz, in her arms. Which left just him and Jacob—the youngest and the eldest brothers—one too irresponsible for marriage and the other so married to his job that Jacob was probably going to end his thirties single.

Again, the curve of Erica's smile filled his mind, followed by the impetuous grin of her son. He pushed them both away and trudged on, pushing his pain-filled body through the rain and mud, step by step, knowing there wasn't much he could do now but walk and pray. Rocks rose tall and jagged on every side. Thick trees pressed in around him. Knowing in his head that he was several hours' drive away from roads or civilization was one thing. But imagining anyone finding him and rescuing him out here was near impossible. He was all on his own, at least for now, and he'd never much been a fan of being left alone with his thoughts. But here he was.

"Once you start playing a role, it's always easier to keep playing it than to stop" was something his brother Trent had told him once. Nick had asked how he'd managed to stay undercover for so long, living a life that wasn't real and keeping himself from ever developing the kind of connection Trent now had with Chloe. So then, what had Nick's role been? Back in high school Erica's brother had played the loud-mouthed lout. Was Erica right in saying Tommy no longer played that role now? Clark had been the golden boy, the good and righteous one, the valedictorian who'd gone on to become Ontario's youngest Member of Provincial Parliament, while successfully killing every sleazy and unseemly rumor that had swirled around him. And while Nick had always suspected the slick and shininess of Clark's whole shtick was an act, it had been one Clark had kept up his entire life, spun into an ambitious career and then died with.

And what role had Nick played exactly? The one who was too much trouble to bother with? The one too difficult to love? Maybe he'd been the one determined to prove Erica was wrong in choosing to love him. This time, he didn't fight it when her face entered his mind, along with an ache that pressed at his chest like a balloon expanding inside his heart. He'd tried hard to forget Erica, if he was honest. He'd had a smattering of very short-term relationships with women he'd met on base—all good, nice and kind women that he'd never been able to make a connection with. Instead he'd always known something was missing, but had never been ready to admit to himself the missing piece was that none of those women was her.

Nothing had ever compared to the connection he'd had with Erica.

And yet he'd never told her how much he'd liked her and cared about her back when they were dating. He'd never even called her his "girlfriend," even though it had been obvious to everyone with two eyes that she had been and, as much as he'd known, on one level, how deeply she was waiting to hear him acknowledge it. No, instead they'd just been "really good friends" and they'd just "hung out."

Just like the moon and the sky were good friends.

Just like the sea hung out with the shore.

They'd sat beside each other in every class since tenth grade and walked home together every afternoon. They'd gone shooting, hunting, climbing, kickboxing and swimming. They'd studied together, although that was usually her rescuing him with some last-minute cramming for a test or helping on an assignment he'd forgotten. He'd invited her over for so many family meals and there'd been something in the warmth in which his parents had spoken to her that it was almost like they'd begun to think of her as an honorary daughter.

Their hands had touched and then eventually their lips, until feeling her arms tossed around him in a quick hug hello and a quick, furtive kiss goodbye had become as habitual to him as breathing. So of course everyone had assumed they were a couple and that he was every bit as serious about her as she was about him. Every now and then one of their friends would haul him aside and tell him that if he didn't step up and make a commitment, he risked losing Erica to someone who would.

But he'd figured he was in the clear as long as she wasn't complaining about the fact he was somehow always unable to commit to plans in advance or that he'd tell her they'd do something and then either not show up or cancel at the last moment. He'd told himself they were too young for a relationship and that he'd make it official when they were sixteen, then seventeen, then eighteen. He'd told himself that the fact Erica never took him by the collar and said, "Hey, are we dating?" meant he was fine never asking himself how he felt about her or what he was willing to do about it.

Then her brother had planned some stupid party that just happened to be on the anniversary of the day Faith had been abducted and killed. Nick had been in a bad mood. He'd had a fight with Erica over the fact that she'd tried to get Tommy to shut the party down. She'd made it clear to Nick that she'd expected him not to drink like her idiot brother, because he knew better than that. Somehow that had made his mood even worse. Not because he'd intended to drink anything or because he'd wanted to be at the party, but because he didn't like anyone telling him what to do. So he'd brushed her off and told her he'd needed some space. She'd left him alone at the party, in a bad mood, surrounded by fools. Then Tommy had started mouthing off. Nick had said stupid things back. They'd traded a few blows, and the next thing he knew, Tommy, Clark and some of their buddies were forcibly kicking Nick out of the party.

Nick had stormed off. He'd hated everything about himself and his life. He'd been yelling and stomping around in the family barn, then turned around to see Erica standing in the doorway, her eyes wide with concern, her heart open enough to listen and care.

Suddenly he'd known, with every beat of his childish heart, just how much he'd cared about her, wanted to marry her and how he didn't deserve her. But somehow, instead of telling her any of that, he'd told her about his big sister who was murdered. Erica'd always known, of course. Everyone did. But she'd also known it was something he'd never been willing to talk about. That night it all spilled out—how he'd grown up knowing he had a big sister who'd been assaulted and murdered when she was twelve and walking home from school, how her killer had never been caught and how her death had torn the family apart.

He'd confessed stuff to her that he'd never told anyone, while she'd hugged him and kissed away the tears he wouldn't let himself shed. He'd told her he'd been born into a hurting family, mourning the loss of someone he'd never met. He'd told her he'd felt guilty for being alive and that his life would never matter enough. That he'd never be as loved as she was, so he'd done everything in his power to push people away, to test the limits of just how much anyone was willing to love him.

And when I lost her, You were there for me, Lord. His thoughts turn into prayers as his feet trudged on through the darkness. *I promised You I'd be a better man and You stood by me every day while I became that man. I just wish I hadn't done it without her. I just wish I hadn't pushed her away. Please, protect Erica and Zander. If she was anyone else I'd wonder if Zander is mine. But I just can't believe she'd ever keep something like that from me—*

The prayer trailed off in his heart as he heard the sound of a motor roaring and cycling in the air above him. Then he saw a light, shining above him, cutting through the rain and swinging back and forth as if looking for someone. But Trent had said no pilot in their right mind would fly in a storm like this...

"Hey!" he shouted and waved his hands over his head, wondering if the flares he had would survive the storm if he tried to light them. How were they ever going to hope to land in terrain like this? "Hey! Hey! Over here!"

A helicopter rescue basket tumbled from the sky toward him. Well, then. Nothing ventured, nothing gained. And he doubted anyone's criminal master plan involved finding a lone soldier in the middle of nowhere and offering him a lift to safety. He climbed into the rescue basket and tugged the rope. It rose and, for a moment, he swung through the air, the basket beating against the trees as he climbed higher and higher toward the helicopter above.

A tall man with broad shoulders, a dark leather jacket and helicopter headset leaned forward. His face was hidden by the light shining behind him.

"Hurry up, bro!" a voice boomed, strong and reassuring, over the din of the engine and motors. "What did I tell you about keeping me waiting when I gotta pick you up?"

No way... It couldn't be...

"Jacob?"

The oldest of the Henry brothers and the man with the hugest heart of anyone Nick had ever met, reached out a strong hand toward him. *Thank You, God!* Nick grabbed it and let his big brother haul him into the rescue helicopter. Nick scrambled onto the floor and pulled himself into a seat as Jacob tossed him a headset. He slid it on.

Jacob slapped twice on the back of the pilot's seat. "We got him!" he shouted.

"You sure?" Max leaned back from his position at the controls, and Nick was suddenly thankful the helicopter paramedic had finally gone for his pilot's license. Max's eyes twinkled as that teasing million-watt grin crossed his face. "I mean that guy could be anyone."

Jacob yanked the basket in and closed the door. "Yup, I think I grabbed some random, soaking, muddy dude out of the woods."

"Well, as long as he doesn't try to hog all the bacon like our little brother does," Max laughed.

Jacob buckled himself into a seat across from

Nick and tossed him a towel. The helicopter rose. "Fun fact, this is how Mom and Dad got you in the first place. We just dropped a random basket out the rear of the station wagon and when we pulled it back there was a baby in it. That's why your middle name is Moses."

"You guys are hi-lar-i-ous." Nick ran the towel over his face. The comforting sound of two of his older brothers laughing filled his ears. He chuckled along with them. The words *What are you doing here?* might've crossed his lips if the two men who'd come to his rescue had been anyone but fellow Henrys. Probably followed by "Do you have any idea how dangerous it is to fly in weather like this?" But if there was one thing he knew about being a Henry it was that they were there for each other, through thick and thin, and had never been ones to let a deadly storm or a crew of gun-toting criminals get in their way.

Trent and Chloe had leaped into action to put their lives and careers on the line to save Max's Daisy when she'd been accused of murder and kidnapping. The entire Henry clan had armed themselves and banded together when the criminals who'd discovered Trent's real identity had come to the family's door to abduct and torture him. Nick had even driven Trent through the night to save Chloe's life from a madman. Rescuing each other was kind of a family tradition. If one of his brothers had been stranded in a storm, Nick would've been the first to commandeer a helicopter, plane or nuclear sub to bring him home.

"You never could stay put and do what you're told, could you, Nick?" Jacob asked. He shook his head. "Trent tells you to stay put and wait to be rescued. Instead you take some undercover cop's motorcycle and go chasing down the tracks to single-handedly stop a train."

Nick ran his hand across the back of his neck. Every part of him was sopping. "First, Liam Bearsmith wasn't an undercover cop, he was a real estate consultant," Nick said, and Jacob snorted loudly. "Second, I would've succeeded if I hadn't been shot at. A lot. The real question is, what took you so long?"

"Maybe we wanted to give you the benefit of the doubt to see if you succeeded on your own." Max's chuckle rumbled through his headset. "I'd hate to ruin your dramatic moment by arriving too early. Then again, you could be impressed that I got here so quickly. Or that I talked someone at the airport in Moosonee into letting us take off."

Laughter seemed to echo and vibrate through the helicopter as it rose above the trees. Nick was beyond relieved. Not just for the rescue. But for the reminder there were people who believed in him and supported him.

God, I can't thank You enough that these are my brothers and I was born into this family.

"Please tell me the front of the train has been stopped and that Erica and her son are okay."

"Sorry, bro. I really wish I could." The smile fell from Jacob's face. Nick wasn't surprised. After all, it had only been twenty minutes since he'd been tossed from the motorcycle. But still, the reminder that Erica was in danger cut him to the bone.

Jacob leaned his elbows on his knees and looked across at him. "The situation is still evolving, and information is scarce. As you know, Max and I have been doing some rescue drills around James Bay…" Yeah, Nick did, but he didn't know why. Much of Jacob's work as a detective was even more secretive than Trent's work. One day, the eldest Henry boy would have to tell him what he'd spent all these years working on. "We got a call from Trent explaining that the train you were coming up on had been hijacked and that you were probably going to be going off after the front half."

"When?" Nick asked.

"The second he got off the phone with you," Jacob said. "He knew you'd find a way and weren't about to stay put. Two rescue trains were dispatched, one heading north to find the rear part of the train, and one heading south from Moosonee to find the front portion."

Nick blinked. "How could they possibly lose the front half of a train?"

"It obviously switched tracks at some point," Jacob said. "So now all they can do is search all the tracks and sweep the area when the storm clears until they find it. Then when they do, they'll set up a blockade in front of the train, force it to stop and negotiate for the hostages' safe release."

The helicopter shook and shuddered as it was buffeted by the wind and storm outside. It dropped a few feet, taking Nick's stomach with it. He was suddenly reminded that Max had crashed the first bird he'd ever solo piloted. They wouldn't be able to fly around in the storm for long.

"So basically all the options are bad ones,"

Nick said. "They can't find the train. When they do find it, they have to force it to stop, basically risking everyone's life. And once it's stopped, they get to negotiate for Erica's and Zander's lives with armed killers."

"Pretty much." This time it was Max who spoke. The smile was gone from his voice, too. "They haven't even managed to establish contact with the hostage takers yet to find out what they want."

"They're thieves," Nick said. "What they were after was a laptop from North Jewels. And they were willing to hijack a train and kill a Member of Provincial Parliament over it."

"Clark Lemain," Jacob supplied. "How many hostages are there?"

"Three maybe four," Nick said. "Erica Knight, her son, Zander, and her brother, Tommy, that I know of. She also suspects the engineer, Bob Bass, might've been forced or coerced into driving the train. We can't discount that he's a hostage, too. Look, guys…"

He took a deep breath. His bothers exchanged a glance. Yeah, being his brothers, they knew what he was going to say before he did. "We have to find that train and then you've got to get me inside it. I can protect the hostages while you alert the authorities to its location and get this bird out of the storm before it tosses us all into a lake. I can negotiate. I'm a military corporal. I have all the necessary training. And the authorities need someone on the inside to let them know what's going on." He leaned forward. "Come on, guys. You don't have to tell me that it's risky, foolish or dangerous. We all know that. But so was coming to find me to begin with, and we also know that this is the best opportunity we have to get the hostages home alive."

Jacob ran his hand over his jaw. Max glanced back and met Nick's eyes.

"Come on, Max," Nick said. "What would you do if Daisy and Fitz were on that train?"

"You know the answer to that," Max said. "They are Henrys. They are family. And we stop at nothing to protect family. Are you telling us that Erica Knight and her son, Zander, are your family?"

Max's voice was as sharp, strong and as pointed as a javelin aimed at Nick's heart. Nick glanced at Jacob and saw the same qualities in his gaze. It was like his brothers knew and saw something they were waiting for him to face. And suddenly Nick heard Erica's adage in his mind.

People are really good at not seeing what they don't want to see... And if she were anyone other than Erica, I'd have asked her if Zander was mine. But Erica has always been on this pedestal in my mind. I can't imagine she'd ever keep something like that from me. I know I need to ask her. But I don't even know how...

"I don't know," Nick said. He shrugged. "After everything I put Erica through, I have no right to even hope for any kind of relationship with her. All I know is that I'm going to fight for them as if they were every bit a Henry as you and me."

The rain had lightened. Erica dozed, lying uncomfortably on one of the seats in the first-class lounge, Zander curled up on top of her. Her limbs ached. But it was nothing compared to the ache in her heart and the bitter taste that fear had left in her mouth. She fought the urge to shift her limbs and instead just thanked God that she'd finally managed to get Zander calmed down after the motorcycle had crashed. The train was moving quite a bit slower than usual, as if wherever they were going the engineer wasn't in a hurry to get there. The lounge had settled around her, into a tableau that was both tedious and tense. Julie stayed hunkered over the laptop while Mr. Grand paced behind her. Lou sat hunched in a chair on the opposite side of the aisle, with a weapon at the ready. Quiet stretched around her, thin and brittle, as if everyone was on edge but no one quite had a handle on how or why. It was like being stuck inside a movie scene just moments before the shark attacked the boat or the earthquake hit, where the only thing to focus on were the tiny little details.

Her eyes were drawn to the deep, wrinkled lines between Mr. Grand's eyes. Something was wrong. For a man who'd seemed so utterly in control when he'd first smoothly pulled a weapon on her, he now seemed uncertain. No, more than that. He seemed downright worried. She saw that same unease in Julie's face and the way her eyes kept glancing instinctively in the direction of the front engine. No doubt whatever she and her brother, wherever he was, had thought they'd signed up for, it wasn't this. Or at least, it hadn't turned out how they'd expected.

Okay, all useful information. But what did it mean? And what did she do about it?

"I'm sorry." Julie glanced up at Mr. Grand. Her voice was low and strained, but still Erica barely managed to make out her words. "I've searched everything I can access. There are no bank account numbers. No financial details. No list of names. There's nothing here."

"Then look harder," Mr. Grand snapped. "There has to be."

And who'd told him that exactly? Someone within North Jewels Diamond Mine? Someone in Clark's office who he'd confided in? Who had hired Mr. Grand to intercept this secretive cloak-and-dagger handoff? What if Clark had been set up? What if there never had been any data on the machine? Why had the train slowed? Why had she only seen three of the thieves? Where was Julie's brother, Rowan? Was Bob being held hostage, and if so, how were they forcing him to drive the train? For that matter was Julie even still a willing participant in this?

Had Nick survived the crash?

How would this all end?

She could feel defiance bubbling up inside her. The desire to fight back beat like a drum in her chest. She lived, breathed and worked on this train. The people they'd left bound and helpless on the side of the tracks had been her coworkers. Clark had been her brother's friend since elementary school. There had to be something she could do. There had to be some way to fight back. She could find something to use as a weapon. She could wait until the next time Mr. Grand went into the front engine or a first-class sleeper cabin and rush Lou. There had to be something, anything, other than just sitting there as hostages.

She glanced at Tommy. He was lying on his back, looking up at the ceiling, his face awash in guilt and misery. Her brother had never backed down from a fight. It'd been his biggest fault for as long as she'd known him, leaving her to clean up his messes, come up with his bail money and make sure he still had a roof over his head. He'd got them into this mess. How could he just crumple and let the villains take over now?

Zander shifted in her arms. His small hands slid up around her neck, holding her tightly. "Mommy, I'm tired. I want to go home. When can we go home?"

"I don't know, Little Soldier."

Tears filled her eyes and she wondered if today would be the day she'd finally let them fall. The little boy in her arms was the most important thing in the world. His life was why she couldn't risk fighting back. She couldn't risk him getting hurt. She couldn't put him in danger. What if she managed to disarm Lou but a stray bullet hit Zander in the process? What if she got free but lost everything? The weight of his little body and her love for him pressed against her chest.

Help me, Lord! I feel both stronger and weaker than I ever have before. I don't know what to do! I don't know how to protect my boy. I don't know how to save him. I'm frightened. I'm exhausted. I need help, Lord. I can't do it alone.

She'd always been responsible for someone, as long as she could remember, long before Zander had come along. After her father had died on an overseas deployment, she'd worked a part-time job in high school to help her mother with the mortgage. She'd kept the house clean when her mother worked long hours. She'd done Tommy's chores and basically been the buffer between the brother who was always popping off about something and their exhausted, overworked mother.

Maybe that was part of why she'd liked Nick

so very much. He'd been easygoing, he'd been independent and able to take care of himself. Nick hadn't put any demands on her. He hadn't asked her for anything. And sure, she'd helped him with studying, but he'd never asked for it or made it feel like it would be her fault if he failed. No, Nick had been his own independent man even when they'd been in junior high together. And she'd been so exhausted from taking care of her mother and brother that she'd loved and craved those moments together when she could just be with Nick, be herself, relax and be free.

But hadn't she been bailing him out, too, in her own way? Maybe she'd never done his dishes, completed his homework or given him money. But she'd let him get away with acting like he didn't care and they weren't together. And why? Because she'd liked him too much to risk losing him. Because she'd been too afraid that if she called him on his nonsense, he'd decide he was happier and better off without her. Because she'd secretly been terrified of losing him.

And she'd lost him anyway.

Lord, I thought I was so strong, not needing him to love me or call me his girlfriend. But maybe I was just an emotional coward. Maybe I didn't believe I was strong enough to lose him. I blamed him for everything. I blamed him for not loving me enough to make our relationship official. When I was never brave enough to face rejection. I blamed him for leaving, when I never had the courage to ask him to stay.

Nick's soft, warm grin filled her mind. And suddenly she was so swept up in the memory of him—the shape of his mouth, the touch of his hand, how the smell of him filled her senses when he wrapped his arms around her—that it was like he was there beside her in the train. A deeper ache moved through her until it even hurt to breathe. She'd missed Nick every day they'd been apart. Now he'd landed back into her life only to be yanked away again.

God, please, let Nick be all right! Please, he needs to be safe! I need to see him again. I need to tell him about Zander. I have to tell him I'm sorry.

Light filled the window above her, bright and glaring, filling her eyes with blinding radiance as if waking from a dream.

Mr. Grand leaped to his feet and shouted for everyone to get down. Julie screamed. Lou yanked his weapon and ran down into the cabin, gun held high as if not knowing where to aim. And still the light shone, not like the tiny pinprick of light of the motorcycle before. But like a giant, celestial spotlight sweeping the night for them. Then she heard the sound of rotors, growing louder and louder as the helicopter came closer.

Hope leaped in her chest. Zander squirmed and struggled in her arms. "I need to see out the window!"

She wrapped her arms around him. "No, you need to stay with Mommy!"

"It's a helicopter!" Lou's voice bellowed. His face reappeared in the front engine.

The noise grew louder. The light grew brighter. The helicopter was getting closer.

"Fire at them!" Mr. Grand ordered. "Shoot them down!"

"With a handgun?" Lou shouted. "You expect me to take down a helicopter with a handgun? I'm not armed for this! Any of this!"

"You got a better idea?" Mr. Grand snapped.

"I do!" Erica said. "Hail them!"

She jumped to her feet, clutching Zander to her chest. Her gaze fixed on Mr. Grand and she hoped her hunch about him was right. If he was lost and floundering, maybe she could convince him. And if he wasn't, at least she could buy whoever was in the helicopter some time. "Look, it's probably a rescue helicopter. It's been half an hour since you left the back part of the train. Clearly someone was going to figure out something was wrong and send someone to find us! This is your opportunity to tell them what you're doing and how this ends!"

And tell me whatever you can about what's going on, so I can figure out what I need to do to get out of here alive...

Lou glared. But she ignored him. Somehow she doubted he was the mastermind who'd hired Mr. Grand.

"Look, it's been about two hours since you hijacked this train," she said, "and less than two until we reach Moosonee. Now, I don't know what your plans are. I'm guessing your plan was to pull whatever data you could off the laptop before we get there, and then what? Walk off calmly and disappear into the sunrise? Because clearly that's not going to happen now. They're going to be sending police and military to intercept the train. They're going to come looking for us. They're going to want to know what your demands are and why you've hijacked this train."

I'm counting on the fact you don't know.

The rotors were so close the noise was almost deafening inside the metal train. Mr. Grand paused for a long moment. Something flickered behind his eyes and, for a moment, she thought he was listening. Then his head shook.

"Please, just let me into the front engine," Erica said. "Let me talk to Bob. I can help him hail the helicopter. You can find a way to end this."

Instead, Mr. Grand shoved his gun into Julie's hands. "Shoot them if they try anything."

He turned, stormed to the end of the first-class car and yelled at Lou to fire. Bullets echoed in the night.

Erica shook her head in frustration. Didn't they realize how impossible their situation was? How hard it was getting themselves deeper, deeper into trouble until there was no way any of them would be able to make it out alive?

"Please, Julie!" Erica turned to the young woman sitting behind the laptop. "Listen to me. They're distracted right now, and I don't know how long we have. We have to get up, run into the front engine and find a way to hail the helicopter. Your brother is in there, right? Holding a gun on the engineer? He won't shoot his sister. He'll listen to you. We can work together to end this. My father was military. My grandfather was military." *And so is my son's father.* "You think once word gets out that a train has been hijacked in northern Ontario they're not going to do something?"

Julie's head shook. Erica took a step forward and reached out her hand.

"Hand me the gun, Julie. Come with me and help me stop the train," she said. "You don't have to fight this battle anymore. We'll figure something out. We'll find a way to end this where nobody gets hurt. Trust me. Your life and your brother's life are worth more that whatever payday you think you're getting. Please, don't be this person when you have the opportunity to be someone better."

There was a thud above her, like something had hit the top of the train. She held her breath. Then suddenly the sound of the rotors began to fade. The helicopter was rising. That was it? The helicopter was leaving? Their rescuers were going?

"No." Julie gritted her teeth. "This ends when I crack the files." Then her slender shoulders drooped as a long sigh moved through her body.

Erica slumped back against the wall, feeling the coolness of the window against the back of her head. *Lord, I don't even know what to pray right now...*

There was a tap, so faint she barely heard it, on the window right beside her head. She glanced back. A cry rose to her lips.

Nick's wet, bedraggled and upside-down face filled the window.

NINE

Erica gasped as suddenly her legs felt so weak she nearly pitched and fell. She grabbed the wall for support.

"Everything okay?" Tommy asked. His eyebrows rose.

What? No! She opened her mouth but no words came out. *How could he ask that? Nick was stuck, flying through the night, on the outside of a train!*

She turned back. Nothing but darkness filled her gaze. Nick's face was gone from the window. She blinked. Had she been imagining it? Or had her body blocked everyone else from seeing his face in the window? Tommy clearly hadn't seen it and not a muscle had moved on Julie's face. She allowed herself one last glance at the window and almost laughed. Four squiggly and smudged letters ran in the condensation

on the outside of the window. She watched as
in an instant the rain wiped them away.

KISH—Keep. It. Simple. Henry.

A hysterical giggle leaped to her lips and she
barely managed to swallow it back.

Nick—*her Nick*—was somehow outside,
clinging to the top of the train. She had no idea
how he'd managed to pull that off. But he was
right—she had to keep it simple. The only thing
that mattered now was helping him get inside
the train.

And that would be anything but simple.

The thought of Nick clinging to the roof of
the train like some kind of superhero made her
both want to laugh and cry. She hadn't told
him about Zander because she was afraid if
Nick knew Zander was his son, he'd do something reckless. And now, here, he'd done the
most reckless and dangerous thing she could
imagine to save them. If there was any man
on the planet tenacious enough to somehow
drop from a helicopter onto a hijacked train in
a rainstorm, it was Nick Henry. Now it was up
to her to save him.

She leaned down to set Zander back onto the
floor. She couldn't remember the last time she'd
carried him this much, and her limbs were ach-

ing. Instead Zander wrapped his arms around her neck and his legs around her waist. He leaned in so close to her ear that his whisper shook her eardrum. "We have to open the window, Mommy, and let Soldier Nick in."

She blinked. Zander's eyes were on hers and he was leaning in so close their noses touched. Well, that was definitely a simple solution. None of the train windows opened from the outside and the reinforced glass wouldn't break easily. The first-class lounge windows didn't open and she didn't know how to break one without someone stopping her. Each of the first-class cabins had windows that opened, though. As well as a door that could be locked from the inside. If she could just find a way to talk Mr. Grand into letting her take Zander into one of those and then lock the door behind her, she could open a window from there.

"Come on," she whispered. "We have to go save the soldier. You remember the sleeper cabins?" He nodded seriously. "We need to go into one of them and open the window, and I need your help to do that. Now, do you think you can yell and cry really, really loudly for Mommy? Like, be really naughty and pretend you need a time-out?"

He nodded super seriously. She smiled.

Lord, please may this work...

"I wanna get off the train!" Zander shrieked so suddenly and loudly that even though she'd just asked him to, the volume still viscerally knocked her back a step. His body flailed so hard she nearly dropped him. "I wanna go home! I wanna go home now!"

No! She hadn't meant immediately! She'd meant once she was talking to Mr. Grand. But Zander was five. He'd never been good at waiting and clearly the opportunity to be helpful—or to throw a tantrum or both—had been too much temptation to bear. Okay. Well, now it was happening, and she'd have to roll with it. She barely managed to set him down as he kicked out hard, his tiny feet catching her in her knees. He flopped onto the floor and rolled. His hands pounded the floor like drums. The long whining wail that emanated from his lungs was so realistic she wondered if it was just pent-up anxiety from everything they'd gone through, or if he'd actually tried this trick on her before.

"Hey!" Julie looked up. The gun shook in Julie's hands. "Make that kid stop that racket!"

"Don't be a monster!" Tommy shouted. "The kid's five. It's one in the morning. He's overtired!"

Thank You, God, for Tommy!

"Let me take him to one of the first-class cabins and put him to bed!" Erica's voice rose over Zander's theatrical wails. "You can't expect him to sleep all night here."

Chaos erupted in a cacophony that seemed to fill and echo in the car. Mr. Grand and Lou ran toward them, shouting. Julie was arguing with Tommy. Her son was caterwauling.

Suddenly her mind flashed back to the Knight family kitchen and the daily shouting matches between her mother and Tommy. No wonder she'd spent so much of her childhood escaping to the Henry farmhouse. No wonder a laid-back guy who didn't seem to get worked up about much of anything was the one she'd fallen for.

"He just needs a nap!" Her voice rose, cutting through the noise with the power that only a mother's could. She bent, scooped Zander up and pulled her son into her arms. Then she turned to Mr. Grand, almost able to feel the protective fire flashing in her eyes. "Let me take him and put him to bed in one of the sleeper cabins. You've got the beds right there.

We might as well use them. We're still just as trapped there as we are here! It's not reasonable to expect a five-year-old to stay up all night without having a meltdown. I get that you want eyes on everyone. I really do. But I'm also guessing the last thing you need right now is a child throwing a tantrum."

The noises and voices faded around her. Even Zander's cries had turned to a sniveling whine.

Please, Lord, we need a break and Nick can't cling to the outside of the train forever...

Mr. Grand cut his eyes at Lou. "I'm going to take Julie here and go work in one of the cabins where it's more quiet than this. You stay here with the hostages. If the brat keeps screaming, eventually he'll tire himself out."

No! She gritted her teeth to keep from crying out. That was the opposite of what she'd wanted! *Help me, Lord! What do I do?*

"Don't worry, Mommy." Zander's hands touched both sides of her face. "I'll do it."

Her son's kiss brushed her cheek before she could even realize what he was doing. He slithered from her arms, hit the floor and started running.

"Zander!" she cried. "No! Stop!"

But as she watched, her little boy sprinted

through the car, dodging his uncle's grasp as Tommy reached for him. Where was he going? What did he think he was doing?

"Stop it! Now!" Mr. Grand's hand reached out. He grabbed Zander by the back of his jacket and yanked him back. The boy dropped his weight and wriggled free.

"Grab him!" Mr. Grand bellowed.

Lou's strong form blocked the aisle. He raised his gun. "Stop!"

They wouldn't shoot a little kid, would they? *Oh, Lord, protect him.*

Her little boy dropped to the ground and rolled, slithering on his stomach like a soldier going into a combat roll. Lou's large hands reached for him but, as she watched, Zander shot to his feet and pelted past him into a sleeper cabin.

It was like being stung by hundreds of very wet and angry bees, Nick thought as he clung to the accordion-like section connecting the engine and first-class car. For all the time he'd spent walking through that odd no-man's-land connection platform between two train cars, he'd never stopped to think what it might be like to travel on top of it, wedged with his hands and legs against opposite sides. But, hey, as uncomfortable as it was, at least he wasn't sliding.

Okay, Lord, now what?

How had his brothers even expected him to get inside the train when they'd lowered him in the rescue basket? True, the train wasn't exactly going that fast, due to the storm and the terrain it was traveling through. According to Max, when they'd spotted the train, it had been going half its expected speed and incredibly slowly— for a train. But what might technically be slow on paper still felt plenty fast for someone clinging to the outside. What was worse, the wind and rain had picked up so fiercely by the time they'd reached the train that any hope of evacuating the hostages by basket would have to wait. No, the trip Nick had taken to the train had been a one-way trip.

And somehow he'd managed to convince two of the most responsible men he knew to let him drop from a helicopter rescue basket onto a moving train. He gritted his teeth and almost grinned. Probably because they knew he'd try to find a way to do it with or without their help. True, he'd usually been the one to take the easy way out. But it was like the sight of Erica through the back of the train before he'd crashed the motorcycle, and the knowledge that she and Zander were being held hostage, had somehow strengthened something inside him. He knew without a sliver of a doubt in his heart that there was nowhere else on earth he'd rather be than out there trying to rescue her.

Well, except for the inside of the train.

Okay, Lord, now what?

Thanks to his brothers he now had two guns, some sturdy rope, a first-aid kit, fire starters, even an inflatable life jacket with an emergency light—pretty much everything he could need in a survival situation—in a bag on his back. Everything but a way inside the train.

"Soldier Nick! Hello! Soldier Nick!" Suddenly a voice drifted toward him on the air, faint and yet determined and distilled with hope. No, it couldn't be. He crawled over to the side of the train and looked down and saw nothing. Yet there was Zander's voice, young, strong and unmistakable. "Hello! Soldier Nick! It's me!"

"Where are you?" Nick called back, hoping the ambient noise of storm and train would keep people inside the train from hearing him.

"Over here!" Then he saw what looked like a

window moving and realized two small hands were pounding on a screen. Was it a trap? Could be. But the boy sounded genuinely happy and at least this time nobody was firing at him.

"I see you!" Nick shouted. "Stand back!"

Okay, so all he needed to do was to somehow inch his way around the top of a moving train in the wind and rain to reach a small window that had apparently been opened by a five-year-old, punch out the screen and climb through. No problem.

Help me, God. I'm more worried about letting him down than I am of falling off the train.

Slowly and carefully, Nick edged and inched his way onto the first-class car and across the top, keeping his body as flat as possible. The metal ridges were thicker and better spaced than most rock walls and obstacle courses he'd climbed. But still. He slithered forward, feeling every time he'd complained about having to crawl through mud or under wire on an obstacle course in the rain come back and bite him. He reached the window and leaned forward, gripping the ledge so tightly his fingers ached, and holding on to the train with all his might as he slid his body far enough that he could look inside the window.

"Hi, Nick!" Zander waved at him enthusiastically through the window. Seemed the boy was all alone in a first-class sleeper cabin. Zander clasped a hand over his mouth as if suddenly realizing he should be quiet.

"Stand back!" Nick said.

He pulled himself up, turned around and slid down, feeling with his feet until he found the window. One swift kick and the screen popped loose. His foot slipped and for a moment he thought he was going to fall. But then the toes of his boots found the window ledge. He slid his legs through, pushed off like a kid going down a slide and let himself tumble into the train. A pull-out sleeper chair broke his fall. He looked up. He and Zander were alone in a sleeper cabin. The door was locked. Nick pulled himself slowly to his feet and waited for someone to pound on the door. Nobody did.

Instead, the sound of Tommy's loud and obnoxious shouting seemed to fill the air outside the cabin. Yeah, he'd remembered what it had been like when Erica's brother got worked up for a fight. It was like being berated by an implacable human bullhorn. Tommy was shouting, full volume, launching a full-out verbal assault on even the idea of opening the door.

Other voices were shouting, too. Two men were swearing, one more colorfully than the other. A woman was screaming she couldn't concentrate. Erica was begging Mr. Grand to let her talk to Zander alone.

"Hi, Nick!" Zander's eyes were on his face, shining with excitement. "You made it! I saw you crash your motorcycle!"

Nick held a finger to his lips. Just because Tommy was shouting didn't mean he was about to risk being heard. But suddenly the boy launched himself into Nick's arms. A lump formed in his throat. He sat there, holding Zander tightly. He ran his hand over the boy's head, feeling his curls under his fingers. Zander hugged him back so hard Nick struggled to breathe. Then Zander broke the hug and sat back beside him on the chair.

"I saved you," Zander said very seriously. "I did. I opened the window. But I couldn't move the screen. Then you kicked it." He frowned and swung his legs, as if wondering if he could've kicked it out himself.

Okay, but that didn't answer what he was doing alone in a sleeper cabin.

"How did you get in here?" Nick asked, his voice dropped to a whisper.

"Mommy and I saw you in the window," Zander whispered back. "We knew we needed to open a window. Mommy asked Mr. Grand if she could bring me into a sleeper cabin to sleep. But Mr. Grand said no. So she told me to act like I was being naughty. I got really loud and started shouting, and then I ran. And they tried to grab me. But I got away and ran in here and locked the door. And Lou asked Mr. Grand if he should shoot the door down. Mr. Grand said no, that I wasn't going anywhere, and maybe I'd tire myself out, and at least with me in here it would be quiet. I was very loud. Then Uncle Tommy got very, very, very loud."

There was a quiver to his chin that implied he didn't tend to like it when Uncle Tommy got loud.

"Okay, but now we have to keep our voices very quiet so nobody knows I'm here, okay?"

Zander nodded. "Okay." He said it so quietly the word was almost silent.

"And how is your mommy?" Nick asked gently.

"She's okay," Zander said. "She wanted to open the window herself."

Nick smiled. "Well, I'm sure I'll see her soon enough."

And figure out a way to get them all safely

off the train. But for now he was on the train and with Zander, and the little boy was safe. *Thank You, God, for that.*

He unfolded slowly, stood and closed the window. The shouting seemed to be on the move. He walked to the door and put his eye to the crack just in time to see Lou force Tommy into one of the sleeper cabins and Mr. Grand force Julie into another. Seemed everybody was getting a time-out and breaking down a door to drag out a now-quiet five-year-old wasn't high on anybody's priority list.

He didn't see Erica.

When he turned back, Zander was watching his face. The boy's green eyes seemed to search out Nick's. His chin quivered. Then his mouth moved and he said something so softly that Nick couldn't catch it. Nick crouched beside him. "What did you say, Little Soldier?"

"I saved you," Zander whispered again, only this time his eyes were wide, as if the thought shocked him to the core. "I saved a soldier!"

"You did!" Nick slid a strong hand on his shoulder. "You were very brave and heroic. You're an amazing boy. You saved my life."

Zander bit his lip and then his gaze dropped to the floor.

Nick felt his voice drop. "What is it?"

"I've never been a hero before," Zander said. His chin quivered. "I'm not a 'mazing boy. I'm a mistake."

Something fierce and protective rose inside Nick. His slid a second hand, gently but firmly, on the boy's shoulders. "That's not true. You are an incredibly amazing boy. People are never mistakes. People are people. And people matter. Who even told you that?"

"Nobody," Zander said. His eyes searched the floor. "Nobody ever told me that. But Uncle Tommy gets loud sometimes when he thinks I'm asleep and not listening. Sometimes he's very, very loud."

At least Tommy had enough sense not to say anything like that in front of the boy. But it didn't make it right.

"I'm sorry for what you heard Uncle Tommy say," Nick said. "Your mommy told me your uncle loves you very, very much. Sometimes adults say things they don't mean and shouldn't say. But that doesn't mean he thinks it's true."

Zander's head still hadn't risen.

"He says it's funny that Mommy called me Zander Moses Knight, because my daddy's the one who should've been sent away down the river."

Moses. The words hit him like a punch in the gut. Erica had been the only person he'd ever told his middle name to. And he'd never minded the way his brothers had joked about it because he knew his parents had chosen it as a sign of God's hope and salvation.

"He says my daddy was a stupid jerk." Zander shrugged. His green eyes rose to Nick's face. "He says things about my daddy I shouldn't say."

Nick's heart was beating so hard he could feel it in his throat. He didn't need Zander to tell him what Tommy had said. He could guess what Tommy had said about Zander's father. That he was immature and irresponsible and selfish...

People are really good at not seeing what they don't want to see. Erica's voice floated through his mind, followed by the pointed look in his brother's eyes when Max had asked, "Are you telling us that Erica Knight and her son, Zander, are your family?"

Erica knew. Tommy knew.

And I've known. Somehow I've always known.

I just didn't want to believe Erica would ever keep something like that some me.

He was a father. And the amazing little boy in front of him was his son.

TEN

The train rumbled on. The rain continued to beat against the windows. But Nick sat, frozen, staring into a pair of curious and adventurous eyes, the same green as his own, feeling like someone had taken hold of his heart and turned it inside out.

This boy was his.

This amazing, brave, strong, incredible, daring child who'd risked everything to save both his mother's life and now Nick's was his own boy. He and Erica Knight had a son, a child, together. The most beautiful and amazing woman he knew was the mother of his child.

It was so obvious he should've seen it. The boy's age. The boy's eyes. The things he'd said Tommy had said about the father. The fact that Tommy had never told Nick about Erica's pregnancy.

But he'd been blinded by the pedestal he'd put Erica on. He'd been blinded by how perfect he told himself she was, or maybe how perfect he'd needed her to be, because telling himself he wasn't good enough for her had been a pretty handy excuse for pushing her away.

The idea Erica Knight would've kept something like that from him was worse than the kidnappers or the motorcycle crash or the feeling of clinging to the outside of a train. It was worse than every broken bone and torn ligament he'd ever suffered. He'd never admired, never respected, never cared for or looked up to anyone as much as her. And the fact she'd done this to him was unthinkable.

But right now, for this moment, he couldn't let that distract him from what really mattered.

"Listen to me." Nick locked his eyes onto his son's, feeling a fierce and protective pride well up inside him. "You are not a mistake. You are very special and very precious. You are brave and strong and smart. You are important, you hear me? You are important to your mother and to your family and to God and—" he swallowed hard as he felt his voice break "—to me. You are very important to me. You are the most important boy I've ever met, and I really hope that one day I can introduce you to my family. Because I have three bigger brothers, two sisters-in-law, a new baby nephew and two really cool parents, and I think they'd all agree you're really special, too."

"Really?" Zander's eyes looked into his, so wide, innocent and eager to be loved.

"Really, really." Nick pulled him into a hug. Zander's arms locked around him and squeezed him back. Suddenly, Nick felt almost paralyzed as he was hit by a whole new understanding of what Erica could've been going through. How could he storm the train now? How could he do anything knowing it might put his own son at risk?

God, I... I don't know what to pray right now. I don't know how to process this. I don't know what to think or how to feel. But thank You for everything that has led me here. Now, please help me get Zander home safely.

There was a knock on the door, so strong and firm it echoed in the small room.

"Zander, honey?" Erica called. "Can you open the door for Mommy?"

Nick froze. Was she alone? Was someone holding a gun to her head? If he opened the door, exactly who and what would come bursting through? He glanced through the crack between the door frame and the door. Her large eyes and worried face filled his gaze. She seemed to be alone. But he didn't exactly have a view of much more than just a foot or two in front of the door. Nick put a finger to Zander's lips, warning him to stay quiet. With the other hand, he slowly reached for and unholstered his weapon.

"You go crouch behind that chair, okay?" he whispered. "Promise me you're going to do exactly what I say. Okay?"

Zander's eyes went wide, and he nodded. Okay. There was another knock at the door. Then the door handle rattled.

"Zander?" Erica's voice grew louder. "Are you okay? I need you to unlock the door for me, okay?"

Nick pressed himself up against the wall and slid back the lock. The door opened, and someone began to step through. He leaped, swiftly and smoothly, grabbing them by the arm, swinging them around, pushing them up against the wall and clamping a hand over their mouth. He slid the door closed with one hand and clicked the lock shut. Then he looked down into Erica's face. Dark, beautiful, long-lashed eyes looked up at him over his hand.

"Mommy!" Zander darted out from behind the chair and threw his arms around his mother's waist.

"Sorry," Nick whispered, peeling his hand away from her mouth and stepping back an inch. "I couldn't be sure it would be you or that you'd be alone."

"Lou's standing at the end of the hall," she whispered. Her hand brushed over the back of their son's head, but her eyes were locked on Nick's face with a look that tugged at something far deeper inside him than he was ready to acknowledge. "About three feet away. Thankfully these cabins are pretty soundproof as long as nobody starts shouting.

"Mr. Grand divided us between three of the sleeper cabins and told Lou to shoot anybody who tried anything funny. He seems more exasperated by the situation than anything now and he's really making things up on the fly. I talked them into letting me check on Zander and convinced them I'd have an easier time calming him down if he didn't see any big men with guns. I think they underestimated just how much trouble having to watch a child that young would be. Also, I think I managed to convince them I wasn't going to try anything foolish like jumping out onto the tracks. The longer this situation drags on, the harder it is on everyone, including them. And as far as Mr. Grand knows, I've been a perfectly cooperative hostage."

Right, because Mr. Grand had no idea what she'd done to Orson's nose and that her collapse in the rear engine had been a strategic fake out. Or that anybody who underestimated Erica Knight's capabilities did so at their peril.

Including, apparently, him.

Her eyes were still holding his, searching his, as if she was looking for long-lost treasure behind his gaze. Then, suddenly, she threw her arm around him, buried her face in his chest and held on to him tightly with one arm while the other hand slid down to brush her son's back.

"I've missed you so much," she whispered into his neck. "You have no idea how happy I am to see you here."

Nick felt his entire body recoil and stiffen. No, he couldn't hug her back. He couldn't wrap his arms around her, pull her into his chest and act like everything was all right.

"What happened to you? Last time I saw you,

your motorcycle was crashing. How are you even here? Did you really drop from a helicopter onto a moving train?" Something like wonder or admiration swelled in her voice, accompanying that look that always made him feel like he was invincible, that he could do anything he set his mind to as long as she was by his side. No, he couldn't let himself fall into that feeling again and let it sweep him under. Not now. Not knowing what he knew.

"Yeah." He shrugged. "But in my defense, the train was going really slowly due to the storm. The tracks are under a few inches of water in places. Jacob and Max risked their lives to fly by in a helicopter and pick me up." He pressed a hand against her shoulder and pushed her back a step. "That's the thing about *family*. You can always count on *family* to be there for you."

Had he meant to put as much bite as he did into the word *family*? Maybe. Her eyes widened. Emotions poured into their depths, flooding them with tears—fear, relief and the need to be forgiven.

Two words etched clearly in her gaze. *You know.*

He nodded.

The rap on the door was so hard and fast that the whole cabin seemed to shake.

"Hey!" Lou shouted. "What you doing in there? You got the kid?" The doorknob rattled. "Open the door!"

Erica swallowed hard. "I've just managed to get him calmed down. You tell Mr. Grand if I drag him out now, he'll kick and scream."

Zander nodded fervently as if to show just how willing he was to go along with the plan.

"What's the problem?" A second voice came now. It was Mr. Grand's.

"They're too quiet and she's locked the door. I want to check what's going on in there."

"I got Zander quiet and settled now," Erica said. "I don't want him flipping out again." No answer. It was like the three of them collectively held their breath. "Please! It's not like we're going anywhere. You've got other things to worry about. And I don't want my kid getting hurt because he's getting underfoot and distracting you."

There was a pause so long that, for a moment, Nick wondered if Mr. Grand had walked away. And, if so, where on earth could he have gone? Then he heard Mr. Grand say, "Look, it's a just a woman and a little kid. They're stuck in a room. It's not like they're going anywhere. And I've got way too much to deal with. Just keep an eye on the door. Tell me if it opens."

Footsteps faded. He glanced through the gap in the door. Lou was standing at the entryway of the car. The hall was empty again.

What was that about? This wasn't like any hijacking or kidnapping he'd ever heard of.

Nick untangled himself from where he was standing between Erica and Zander. "Come on. Let's move away from the wall. The last thing we need is somebody trying to fire through it. I just wish the furniture wasn't bolted to the floor so I could wedge something in front of the door."

"They won't," she said, keeping her voice low. "Whatever's going on with this heist, and whatever his plan is, I really don't think Mr. Grand wants to hurt Zander."

Erica shook her head and the scent of her seemed to fill his senses. Suddenly he was very aware of just how small their quarters were.

"That doesn't mean he wouldn't or that somebody else couldn't," he whispered. He couldn't help the graveled tone of his voice.

Despite the anger and the hurt burning inside him, there was still some invisible cord tugging at him, reaching for him, pulling him into her. Like he was held in place by the dark, fathomless eyes of the only woman he'd ever got close to giving his heart to.

At the same time he could feel that old, familiar need to push away. Erica used to joke that every time he'd hugged her or complimented her, he'd always immediately deflect and step back. Well, now he had reason, didn't he? They still hadn't had the conversation. Not out loud. He still hadn't asked the question and she hadn't answered it. And now, despite how hard he'd fought and everything he'd gone through to get inside that train, part of him would've rather climb right back out the window and risk getting dashed to pieces by the tracks than ask her to confirm what he already knew and why she'd kept his son from him.

"What's wrong?" Erica whispered.

"You know," he said softly. "We've known each other too long to play games. Not about something like this."

"I like games!" Zander's voice perked up from the corner of the room.

Nick felt Erica's hand grab his arm and clench. "Please," she whispered, "not in front of Zander."

He swallowed hard. And when were they supposed to talk about it? After they were free and rescued? What if that never happened? What if tonight was all they had? He closed his eyes. *God, help me be the best possible man I can be right now.*

He let out a long breath. Yeah, he should really check in with his brothers. He looked back at Erica. As he watched, a tear slipped from the corner of her eye. She didn't even try to wipe it away. He turned, pulled out the satellite phone.

"You got a spy phone?" Zander asked.

"And two guns," Nick whispered. "One on my belt and one around my ankle. A Henry man is always prepared." Though he couldn't imagine how anything could have prepared him for this.

He turned the volume on the phone as low as it would go, then dialed.

"Hey, Nick!" Relief filled Jacob's voice.

"Told you he wasn't dead." Max's voice sounded in the distance with a laugh.

"What's the good news?" Jacob asked. "You still clinging to the outside of the train?"

Like his brothers hadn't been watching from a safe distance on infrared cameras or would've left him if they hadn't known he was safe.

"Nope, I'm indoors," he said quietly. "Actually, I'm with Erica and Zander right now in a sleeper cabin. Still on the train but completely secure for now."

"Thank You, God," he heard Jacob pray.

Then Max added, "Amen to that."

"Sorry, I've got to whisper," Nick said. "Hopefully you can hear me."

"Everyone okay?" Jacob asked.

"Yup, all good." Nick ran his hand over his jaw, trying to think about all the different definitions of *good* and deciding that "physically alive and currently not being shot at" was close enough.

"We've alerted the powers that be to the train's location," Jacob said. "They're going to set up roadblocks about forty minutes northeast of where you are. Judging by radar, the train is still heading to Moosonee, just by a different route."

Nick wasn't sure what to make of that.

"Actually, can you do me a favor and talk to Zander right now?" Nick asked. "I'm sure he would love to tell you all about his adventures. Plus, we're really short on both time and space right now. If he forgets, remind him we're only using our whisper voices." His eyes cut firmly to Erica's face. "I'd like to have a quick word with his mom without him listening."

Erica blinked hard and wiped her hands over her eyes. But the tears didn't stop. She turned away before Zander could see. All this time, all these years, she'd felt too strong to cry. But the look of betrayal in Nick's eyes when he'd realized Zander was his had broken something deep and central inside her core.

Nick, I'm so sorry. I don't know what to say. But you'd left me. You'd hurt me. I didn't know how to tell you. I didn't know how to trust you.

She opened her mouth but no words came out. He wasn't even looking at her. She watched as he said a few more words to his brother then crouched down and handed Zander the phone.

"Jacob and Max are my big brothers," Nick said. He unrolled a pair of headphones from his pocket and plugged them into the phone. "Jacob's a police detective and Max is a paramedic. He flies a helicopter. You can talk to them like a regular phone and listen to them in the headphones, okay?"

Not that Zander needed much of an explanation or convincing. He scrambled onto the sleeper chair in the corner and pressed the headphones to his ears. "Hi! This is Zander Knight! Over!"

Nick stood there for a long moment, just looking at their son curled up happily on the chair, giggling at whatever Nick's brother was saying. Then Nick straightened and turned toward her, his full gaze falling upon her face. She stepped into the corner of the sleeper cabin, as far away from Zander as possible. Nick stepped closer until his toes were almost brushing against hers.

"You should have told me," he whispered.

"I know." Fresh tears escaped her eyes. Nick just stood there and watched them. "Tommy said he'd told you."

"When? Years ago? And you believed him?"

"I was pregnant! You were gone! My whole life was thrown into chaos."

"How about today?" he asked. "When we were trapped in the baggage car? When we were alone in the back engine? When I almost fell to my knees, apologized for just how badly I'd failed you, told you how sorry I was and begged you to forgive me?"

"You didn't fall to your knees—"

"You have no idea how hard it was for me to stay standing!"

He shook his head and blew out a long breath. But if he was angry, she couldn't tell how much of it was aimed at her and how much at him. His eyes fixed on her face and a look moved through them that was so raw and vulnerable it wrenched something inside her. How had she ever convinced herself she didn't care for this man? It was like every beat of her heart moved in and out in time to his breath.

I like you. I care about you. I want you to be Zander's father. And in my life, too. In my heart and mind, there's only ever been you.

Her hand brushed his arm. "Nick, I was wrong. I'm sorry. I never felt like you cared enough to take a hit for me. I always felt like I was some add-on to your life. I didn't think you'd want to be there for a child. But we can't change the past. We're here now. We're together. Let's just forgive each other and move on somehow."

Had he been willing to take a hit for her? Maybe not. But that didn't justify what she'd done. It didn't justify keeping his son from him. He looked at the ceiling. Then he pulled away.

"You didn't tell me because you didn't trust me," he said. "You don't know who I am now. And I don't know you, either. It's as simple as that. Let's just shelve this whole conversation for now and move on."

"But—"

"We don't have time." He crossed his arms then glanced to where Zander was curled in the corner happily explaining every moment of his adventure in great detail to Nick's, no doubt bemused, brothers. "Tell me everything you know quickly."

"Nick—"

"Here's what I know." He stepped back. "The back half of the train has been secured. There's a rescue operation under way to locate them and find the stranded crew. They're scrambling a team about forty minutes down the tracks ahead of us to try to force the train to stop. It's my goal to keep you and Zander safe before the situation escalates. Now, get me up to speed."

She blinked hard. Her chin rose. Fine, if that was the way he wanted it to be.

"I think there are six other people on this train besides the three of us." Her stance mirrored his. "Tommy is in a sleeper cabin across from us. He's being held hostage but not injured. Julie is trying to hack into the stolen laptop. I'm pretty sure her brother, Rowan, is in the front engine with Bob, who's still driving the train—but I haven't got eyes on them. Lou is waving the gun around. Mr. Grand is really frazzled. I don't think he has an endgame."

Nick blinked. "Explain."

"Clark apparently told Tommy that he was working with a whistle-blower within North Jewels's mining to expose hidden offshore bank accounts and smuggled diamond routes. Clark was going to use it to take down your brother's investigation. Mr. Grand is trying to get Julie to hack the information and make a copy of it before they turn the laptop over to whoever hired them." Nick whistled under his breath. "But Mr. Grand's had Julie searching the laptop for over an hour with a gun to her head and she's found nothing."

"Yeah, that tracks." Nick sighed. "Trent had originally been tagged to go undercover on that operation when he and Chloe realized they'd wanted something very different for their future. Instead, Trent had taken a promotion and been part of the team that'd overseen it from headquarters. Obviously, I don't know all the details, but I don't believe the investigation was faulty. I trust my brother. Frankly this whole offshore accounts and foreign smugglers thing is ludicrous. But the idea that Clark thought he was getting a laptop with that kind of information from a whistle-blower, and that somebody tried to intercept it, fits what we know."

"So, if you think the laptop doesn't contain evidence of offshore accounts and hidden diamonds, then you think Julie and Mr. Grand are searching it for nothing?" Erica asked.

"Huh. Now, that's a thought."

"In which case, Clark was played," she said. "But if he was played, then so was whoever hired Mr. Grand to steal the laptop."

"I still don't think Clark's murder was random," he said. "You said Mr. Grand is frazzled?"

"Yeah. I don't know what he was expecting to happen, but it definitely wasn't how things have gone."

The floor seemed to shift beneath them. The train had slowed even more and was now going uphill.

"Why was the train separated?" he asked.

"That I don't know."

"Why did it change route?"

What? "I didn't know it had!" Her mind scrambled. Changing course meant physically switching the tracks. The only time they stopped long enough for that was to let the crew out. "Someone must've jumped out of the engine and switched the tracks. We just didn't catch it on camera. Where are we headed now?"

"Moosonee still." Nick held a hand up as if to reassure her. "Don't worry. The authorities know where we are. We're just taking slightly different tracks."

Different tracks? Like all tracks were the same. She glanced at the window and saw nothing but darkness. "What was the ground like?"

"I don't know. It's wet."

"How wet? Are the tracks under water? Are there high rocks on either side?"

"Yeah." He nodded.

"Bob should know better!" She ran her hand through her hair. "There's a faster route to Moosonee that will cut almost an hour off the trip. But it's also almost never used because the tracks are older, the terrain is more treacherous and it means crossing a lot of older railway bridges, some of which aren't in the best shape. The river's prone to overflowing its banks, which is bad news for older bridges."

She wanted to pace but there wasn't any room, so instead she just settled for waving her hands.

"Either way, the train is going to be stopped," Nick said.

"Not if it derails first!" She caught her voice just as it was beginning to rise and clamped her hand over her mouth. "Not if we try to cross a railway bridge while the water's too high." Then she glanced at her watch. "If we are on those tracks, we don't have forty minutes. We have fifteen, max, before we have to cross the river. And when that happens, if Bob's not on top of things, this train could derail and get washed away. And I'm not waiting around to see if that's going to happen." She glanced at Zander. His excited monologue hadn't paused for breath. "Tell your brothers to prepare for an evacuation from the borders of Moose River."

"What are you going to do?" Nick asked. "Jump off a moving train?"

"If we have to. It beats drowning in a giant metal tomb."

"Right, and how many times did you tell me off for being impulsive?"

"You jumped off a helicopter!"

"I was lowered from a helicopter! To rescue you and Zander. And I didn't know—" He caught himself abruptly and lowered his voice. "And I didn't know I was a father then."

"You're here to help us escape," she said. "Because you know as well as I do that in a hostage and kidnapping situation every moment you stay in captivity the more dangerous it becomes. It's been two hours now since he stuck a gun into my back. It's been an hour since the train separated. It's time we get out of here by any reasonably safe means possible. Look, I don't like it any more than you do. But I'm telling you that the train is going to get really slow when it crosses the bridge. Plus, from there we'll be walking distance from an abandoned train station where we can ride out the storm and wait for rescue. If all Mr. Grand really cares about is the laptop, then he'll cut his losses and let us go, just like he was happy to jettison Fox, Orson and the back half of the train!"

Nick opened his mouth to argue. Then he shut it again. She was right and she knew it.

"They hung up!" Zander said. She turned to him. He got up slowly. "They didn't even say goodbye. We were talking and there was this static noise like *crush-shush-crush* and then they weren't there."

Erica turned to Nick and suddenly she found herself reaching for him, throwing her arms around his neck and hugging him. He didn't hug her back but he didn't push her away, either. He just stood there and let her hold him.

"Look," she whispered in his ear. "I know that I've hurt you and you've hurt me. But right now you're all I've got and I'm all you've got. We're in this together. Whatever we do, we do it together."

She stepped back. The wheels squealed beneath them. Voices shouted down the hall. They were reaching the river sooner than she'd realized. What was Bob thinking? Only a few more minutes and they'd be out over the water.

"Why don't you go tell them to stop the train!" Zander grabbed Nick's hand. He gazed up at him trustingly. "You can do it. You're a soldier. Just walk into the engine and say, 'Hey! What you're doing is not safe! Or nice! You're going to be in trouble! Stop the train now!'"

Nick blinked. As Erica watched, she could see the gears moving in his head. She wasn't sure what she was seeing, but she recognized something in his eyes. He was making a decision. Then his eyes cut to her face and somehow she knew what he was going to do. "You're telling me that it's not safe to go over the bridge? That if they don't slow down we're going to derail?"

She nodded.

"Okay, then, I'm going to have to go do something really smart and really crazy. You've just got to promise me to keep Zander safe."

"Of course I will," she said softly.

"I know," he said, and the two words spoke volumes He hesitated and for one split second she saw something moved through the depths of his eyes. Something soft. Something strong. Something that shook her to the core and made her think for a moment that he was about to kiss her, right there, in front of their son, and that she was going to let him. Instead he blinked, and the look disappeared. The look vanished. He unholstered his other weapon.

"Wait." She brushed his sleeve. "What are you going to do?"

He gritted his teeth. His jaw set. "I'm going to take this train back."

ELEVEN

Did it still count as hijacking a train if somebody else had hijacked it first? The thought crossed Nick's mind as he slowly unlocked the door. He peered out. The hallway was empty. But he could see Lou's hulking form standing in the doorway at the end of the car. The door between them was closed, but he didn't expect it would be that way for long. It was a straight, open line, with only one direction to go and nowhere to hide. As for taking out his target, he'd be able to hit Lou's left arm from here, but that wouldn't be an easy shot.

Not a lot of options. He might as well be a fish leaping right into a straight and narrow barrel. The only advantages he had were speed and surprise.

He eased the door shut again.

"You must be joking." Erica's hand grabbed his arm. "You can't stop the train."

"Not joking, not even a little bit," he said. He pulled away. "We don't have any other choice. You said it's dangerous for the train to keep moving. You suspect the person driving it is being held hostage. So the only option is for me to go put a gun to Mr. Grand's head and explain very kindly that he's putting people's lives in danger and they need to stop the train."

"But there are more of them than there are of you!"

He felt a grim smile cross his lips.

"Yes, but unlike them I'm not flustered and know what I'm doing." Then he paused and shrugged his jacket off. "Here, put this on. I know it's wet. But I have some rope, an inflatable life jacket, a first-aid kit, emergency food rations and some other stuff. If anything happens, take Zander, find a way off this train and keep him safe."

She nodded and slipped her arms through the sleeves of the wet jacket, looking every bit as adorable as when she used to borrow his clothes back in the day.

"Promise me you'll save Tommy," she said. "He took a swing at Lou to save Zander's life and that gave Zander the ability to get away. Lou hit Tommy pretty bad for that. He tied him up and put him in one of the sleeper cabins, I think. I don't know for sure. If the train derails while he's still inside, he'll drown."

He let out a sigh. That complicated things and the situation was already complicated enough as it was. "He's the only other hostage, right?"

"Yeah. Except for Bob, and it's possible Julie and Rowan might be fed up enough with the situation to bail on Mr. Grand. But I wouldn't count on it."

Tommy had bullied him, punched him, lied to him and about him, actively tried to ruin his life, never delivered Nick's letter to Erica and kept him from knowing about his son. The thing about taking a vow to serve his country, though, was that he didn't get to pick and choose who was worthy of saving.

"I'll do my best to save your brother and anyone else who wants to be rescued. I promise." He bent down and pulled a gun from his ankle holster. Then he handed it to her. Their fingertips touched. His chest tightened and for a moment he wished he could just let go of the pain and tell her he forgave her. But that wouldn't be true and maybe it never would be. "I trust you still know how to use this? When the train stops, or even slows enough that you're able to jump out safely, I want you to take Zander and make a run for it. Don't look back. Okay?"

The train squealed again. Erica's face paled. He turned toward the door and prayed.

Okay, God, help me. This isn't the first time I've drawn my weapon, but it really feels like I'm walking right into an ambush. If this is it for me, please keep Erica and Zander safe. Thank You that I got to meet him... He ended the prayer there but felt one more thought move through his heart.

And that I got to see Erica again.

Then he dived into the hallway and rolled, moving fast, staying low and not wasting a bullet on a shot he didn't know he had for sure. Lou fired above him. He came up by the closest sleeper cabin and yanked the door handle. It was locked. But the bullet sounding above him really didn't give him much time to wonder why. He dived to the right and into the door of the cabin opposite as he felt another bullet fly behind him. This time he crashed through the door and into the sleeper cabin.

Tommy looked up at him. Erica's brother was

alone. His face looked like Lou had got a couple of punches in, and both his hands and feet were tied. His jaw dropped. "Nick Henry?"

Nick could hear Lou pounding down the hall. He grabbed Tommy, yanked him down and to the right, shielding him with his body as Lou flung the door open and fired into the room. The thug got off exactly one shot. It hit the window above them. The glass shattered. Rain and wind coursed through. Lou loaded another bullet into the chamber. But he didn't get the opportunity to fire again.

Nick pushed off Tommy and dived at Lou, catching the criminal low and hard. He fell back into the hallway, taking Nick with him. Nick landed on top of the thug. Lou struggled to regain his grip on the gun. The train shuddered suddenly. The gun clattered down the car. Nick delivered a blow to Lou's jaw and then dived down the train for the weapon. Lou scrambled up, hesitated and then pelted down the train toward the front engine before Nick could even think of getting off a shot.

Not that shooting a man in the back was ever going to be his style. For now he was thankful Lou was running in the opposite direction of Erica and Zander.

Nick slid Lou's weapon into his ankle holster and kept the gun he trusted in his hand. He ran back into the sleeper cabin where he'd left Tommy. Shattered glass covered the floor. Fresh blood seeped from Tommy's lip. Water poured into the train, coursing over Tommy's body. Nick reached to help him but Tommy shook him off.

"So Nick Henry, of all people, has shown up playing the big strong soldier," Tommy said. "Never thought I'd see the day."

"I'm not playing." Nick gritted his teeth. "And I'm not wasting time arguing with you."

He secured his weapon, yanked a knife from his pants pocket and cut Tommy's leg bindings.

"Erica and Zander are safe in the cabin at the end of the hall," Nick said. Then he freed Tommy's legs. "Join them there. I'm going to stop the train and they're going to escape out the back." He reached for Tommy's hand to help him up. "I don't expect you to like me, and I don't have to like you. But we both care about Erica and Zander. Promise me you'll do whatever it takes to keep them safe. Erica's the most incredible person I've ever met and she deserved way better than either of us treated her."

There was a noise in the hallway behind him. Nick gripped Tommy and yanked him to his feet. Then he took out his weapon and stepped into the hallway. A nervous face with long blond hair looked out at him from the door that had been locked. There was a laptop clasped to her chest and a knife in her hand.

"Julie, right?" Nick reached out to her like she was a frightened animal he was afraid of spooking. He was vaguely aware of Tommy scrambling down the hall behind him and Erica letting him into the sleeper cabin. "I'm Corporal Nick Henry, and I'm not going to hurt you. I just want to save the lives of everyone aboard."

Could he trust her with where the others were or what the plan was? No. He didn't want her to run around stabbing anyone he cared about, either. But he could give her the option of saving herself.

"Give me the knife," he said. "When the train slows down, make a run for the back door. The train is probably going to derail at the next bridge. You don't want to be on it when it does. If you leave the laptop behind, they might not even come after us and let us go."

Julie hugged the laptop closer. Her knuckles tightened white around the knife.

"I can't leave without the laptop," she said. "The data on here is worth millions of dollars."

"Yeah, I got that you guys think that," Nick said. "But right now, I honestly don't care what happens to that laptop one way or the other. And I'm not going to stand around and argue with you."

With a quick flick of his hands he flipped the knife from her grasp. It fell to the floor. The laptop clattered after it. She cried out and snatched the laptop back, like it was somebody's baby. She had no idea just how easy it would be for him to take it from her. But it was just a matter of time before Lou came back and Nick had way bigger problems to worry about. "You do what you need to do. Just stay here and stay low. I don't want you getting hit by a stray bullet. When the time comes, I hope you make the right decision."

A gun clicked behind him. He turned, hearing Julie close the door. Lou stood facing him, gun in his hand. Seemed he'd got himself another weapon to make up for the one Nick had taken. Hopefully he'd borrowed it from another thief, which meant fewer armed men ahead.

"Come on." Lou gestured to him. "The boss wants to see you."

Well, that was definitely one way to get into the front engine. It was plan B to charge in on his own accord. But walking into the front engine on his own two feet certainly beat some of the alternatives.

Nick raised his hands. Lou gestured to him to drop the weapons. Nick tossed the guns and let the thug lead him into the front engine.

They walked through the door. But his foot had barely crossed the threshold when Lou hit him on the back of the head. He fell forward and landed hard on his knees. Frustration filled his throat. No, this couldn't be how it ended. He blinked. Young Rowan stood at the train controls. Mr. Grand stood with his arms crossed and a grin on his face. But the forced smugness of his smile was undercut by the worry in his eyes. He didn't see a third man anywhere.

"Where's Bob, the engineer?" he asked. "I thought he was driving the train."

"He got off," Mr. Grand said. "Now, tell me, soldier, how did you stow away on this train?"

"I didn't." Nick felt his grin go tight. "I got dropped off by a helicopter, actually."

Mr. Grand didn't look like he believed him and, for a second, Nick wondered how the thief thought he'd got there and what he thought was really going on.

"I'm here to tell you to stop the train," Nick said. His voice rose. "Rowan here took you on a lousy set of tracks. I'm sure you thought it was a shortcut, or would make it harder to find you or take you closer to wherever you stashed the getaway vehicle. But I don't care. The river is overflowing. The tracks are flooding. You're putting your lives and everyone else's lives in danger. You need to stop the train."

Mr. Grand snorted. But the lines of worry between his eyes never shifted. "Or what?"

Hadn't he been listening? Did he think this was a joke? Nick raised his chin. "Or I'm going to figure out a way to stop this train and save all your lives whether you want me to or not."

Mr. Grand laughed louder and with bite. The muzzle of Lou's gun pressed into the back of Nick's head. "And you really think you could stop the train?"

A bullet cracked behind him. Lou shouted in pain. His gun tumbled to the floor.

"Not without backup." Erica's voice came from behind him. Nick glanced around. Lou was down on the ground, nursing his bleeding hand. Erica pointed Nick's gun squarely and firmly at the young man behind the controls. Her hair fell wild and loose around her shoulders. She was still wearing his jacket. "Stop. This. Train. Now."

Rowan hit the emergency stop. It was one thing to know how abrupt an emergency stop could be, Erica thought. It was a whole other thing feeling the ground yanked from under her and watching the people around her get tossed like bowling pins. Rowan hit the floor. Mr. Grand shouted curses. Lou rolled like a sack of beets.

Erica pitched forward but in an instant Nick's arms were around her. Holding her, keeping her steady.

"Where's Bob?" she shouted.

"Apparently he left." Nick's voice was in her ear. "Where's Zander?"

"I left him with Tommy," she said. The train skidded forward. "Come on. We've got to disarm them and then we've got to run. We could still derail, especially if we don't stop before we hit the bridge."

Okay. He let go of her. She grabbed hold of the door and held the gun, covering him as he quickly patted everyone down, relieving them of their weapons as he went.

"Now, we're getting out of here," he said. "You all can stay on this train, start the engine again and go on with your plan, whatever it is. Or you can give up all this and get off the train before you risk derailing. I'm not the police and I don't care about the laptop. My job is to rescue the hostages. Got it? But I'm not leaving you with any weapons." No answer. Looked like nobody had any common sense in this crew. He turned to Erica. "Let's go." They turned to run.

"You're not getting away with this!" Mr. Grand called. He leaped, Nick spun and caught him with his elbow before he could land a blow. Mr. Grand crumpled to the ground.

"Really?" Nick said. "Don't be that guy. Of all the choices you could make right now, you went for that?" He heard Erica snort. He began to back out of the room. "I really want to tie you up. But I don't want to doom you to drown or die if the train derails. So instead, I'm going to tie the door closed, nice and loose. Hopefully it'll take you just long enough to get free."

Erica and Nick stumbled backward out of the

front engine. She yanked a length of rope from his bag. He tied the door closed.

"What were you thinking?" Nick said. "I told you to stay with Zander."

"Saving your life?" Erica said. "Having your back? How dare the mighty Nick Henry let somebody care about him?"

She felt the words catch in her throat and something fierce flashed in her eyes almost like she was daring him to contradict her or to brush off the words. Instead, as she watched, something softened in his face. He swallowed hard.

"I know," he said. "And I still care about you. Let's go."

She turned and ran into the first-class car and he followed, grabbing hold of the doors and pulling themselves forward, like they were trying to make their way to the top of a sinking ship. Ahead, she could see Tommy standing by the back door, holding Zander tightly in his strong arms. She smiled. Her brother had wrapped the bright yellow life jacket around Zander.

"Once it stops, how long does it take for him to start the train going forward again?" Nick shouted.

"A few minutes. We can wait until the train comes to a complete stop and then jump out."

Hopefully they'd get a decent head start. But as they drew closer, they could hear Tommy shout.

"We got a problem!" Tommy shoved the door open. And as she stopped and looked out into the darkness, a deep roar filled her ears. Moose River. "We just crossed onto a bridge. We're over the river. I can't even see the tracks."

Save us, Lord! Erica stood at the back of the train and took a breath. The train shook. Water buffeted them. They could still derail. "The water can't be more than a few inches deep. If it was, the train wouldn't run. We have to jump and trust the rails are there."

"Mommy!" Zander reached out of her brother's arms and squeezed her shoulder. "You saved Nick!"

She felt Nick's hand reach for hers. She took it and let her fingers tighten in his.

"We saved each other," she said. "Now, come on, Little Soldier. We're going to jump."

"Wait for me!" A female voice rose in the air behind her.

Erica turned back as Julie burst through the

door of the sleeper cabin and ran for them, clutching the laptop to her chest.

"Welcome to the party," Nick called. "I hope you can swim."

The air cracked. Erica didn't see where the bullet had come from, all she knew was that gunfire sounded.

Julie fell, barely having a chance to open her mouth let alone scream as the bullet flew through her chest. She fell lifeless to the floor, and Erica glanced back, thankful to see Tommy had shielded Zander's eyes from the woman's death. The laptop dropped, sliding across the floor, slipping out the door and falling into the night. In an instant it was swallowed up by the river and gone.

"Where did that shot come from?" Nick asked.

"I don't know." Fear rose in Erica's throat. They had to jump. "I thought you got everyone."

Another bullet flew. She pressed herself against the wall. Tommy shouted as his left leg collapsed like someone had swept it out from under him. Her brother fell, backward off the train, her son still tight in his arms.

"Zander!" Her son's name slipped in a scream through her lips.

For a split second she watched as Tommy hit the water, blood seeping from his leg. She saw Zander's eyes, full of fear, reaching for her. "Mommy!"

She jumped into the water after him. But it was too late. Her baby boy was ripped from his uncle's arms, the river yanking him downstream. His cries filled the air.

Her son was gone.

TWELVE

It was like two bullets piercing Nick's heart at once in a moment—the sight of his son disappearing in the dark black waters and the anguished cry of terror leaving Erica's lips.

"Stay with your brother!" he shouted, leaping onto the train tracks. "I'll get Zander!"

He dived off the bridge and into the water, feeling all the words he'd wished he'd said swirling around him.

I forgive you. I missed you. I loved you. I think maybe I still do.

Cold black depths swept around him, yanking him under in an instant. He fought forward and pressed his body through the cold, letting the current sweep him down the river, downstream toward his son.

Lord, I will give You anything. I will live any

life You call me to. Just, please, let me save my son.

He surfaced and gasped for breath. Rain beat against him. His body swirled in circles. Behind him he could see the lights of the train sliding off the tracks. It hit the end of the bridge and toppled. The deafening screech of rock and metal filled the air as the train derailed on the opposite shore. *Thank You, God.* Hopefully no one on board was seriously hurt. He swam with the current.

"Zander!" He shouted his son's name into the night. "Zander! Where are you?"

He heard nothing but the roar of the river and the beat of the rain. His chest ached like his heart was splitting open. Rain and tears lashed his face as he half swam and was swept helplessly downstream.

If only he'd been a better man. If only he'd figured out what he'd wanted sooner. If only he'd—

A light flickered. Small in the distance. A tiny little pinprick of light. On and off and on again.

SOS. SOS.

The life jacket's emergency light! Hope surged like fire through his heart.

Zander!

"Hold on! I'm coming!" He pressed his body through the water, despite the rain, despite the wind, despite the weight of his boots dragging against his legs and the fatigue in his arms. He swam for his son, shouting Zander's name into the storm.

Until he heard his faint voice, a faint voice floating back toward him. "Nick! Help! I'm here!"

A breath later Nick caught up to him. He reached for his son, wrapped his arms around him and pulled him into his chest. Relief exploded through his heart as he felt Zander's arms latch around him and pull him in with a force that nearly stole Nick's breath from his throat. For a second, father and son swirled in the water together.

"I've got you," Nick said. "You're safe. I've got you."

He held the boy against him and pulled them toward to shore, kicking and swimming with one arm. He pushed against the current and through the water until he felt the dirt under his feet, then rocks smacking his shins and then the rough scrub of bushes and branches against his hands. He latched his hand around a thin tree and yanked himself and Zander out of the water and onto the shore. He collapsed on the ground, cradling Zander in his arm. For a moment they lay there, staring up at the rain. Darkness surrounded them, punctuated only by the flickering of Zander's little SOS light.

"You…you…you saved me…" Tears stuttered through Zander's voice. "You picked me out of the water just like Moses."

"Of course I did." Nick sat up slowly and helped Zander sit up, too. "I will always come for you. No matter where you go. Are you hurt?"

"No, but I'm wet." Zander shook his head. "And I was really scared."

"So was I," Nick admitted.

Tears overtook Zander's voice. He started to cry, throwing his arms back around Nick and holding him so tightly Nick felt tears fill his eyes.

"I will never lose you or give up on you," Nick said. He ran his hand over the back of his son's head. "You hear me? You are important. You are loved. No matter what you do or where you go, no matter how far away you get or how long we go between seeing each other, no matter what—I will always love you. I will always protect you. I will always have your back. And I will always be there for you. No matter what. I promise. Now, come on. We've got to go find your mommy."

He pushed his exhausted limbs to stretch. They climbed the bank and started walking, the long, hard walk back toward the railway bridge, using the light of the lifejacket's emergency flashlight to guide their steps.

"Zander!" Erica's voice burst out at them from the distance.

"Mommy!" Zander cried.

Nick saw Erica running toward her son and then Zander running full tilt toward his mother. He hung back, watched and waited, as son and mother flung themselves into each other's arms and tumbled to their knees together, where they hugged, laughed, cried and prayed.

Thank You, Lord. Please, whatever it takes, help me be there for them. May I never let either of them down ever again.

Then, eventually, he saw Tommy limp up behind them. He was leaning on a thick branch as a crutch. A makeshift tourniquet was wrapped around his leg for the bullet wound. But it looked like the blood had stopped and he could still put some pressure on it. Thankfully, it seemed the wound wasn't too serious.

Erica eased her arms loose enough to let Zander hug his uncle.

"I'm sorry, Little Soldier," Tommy gasped. "I'm so sorry."

"It's not your fault, Uncle Tommy!" Zander said. "Somebody shot you!"

Nick turned and walked off to give them privacy. But he felt Erica's hand on his arm, pulling him back. He turned toward her.

"Thank you." Two words slipped from her lips that somehow said more than a thousand ever could. "You saved my—our son..."

"Thank you for trusting me to save him," Nick said. His eyes rose to the sky. But still he could feel her there, standing in front of him, as if the space between them had disappeared. "Look, I know I haven't always been the most reliable, and I know you've had your reasons for not trusting me in the past. But when Zander's life was on the line, you stayed on the bridge with your brother and trusted me to swim for him. That means everything to me."

"I..." She swallowed hard. "Look, Nick, I..."

"Let me go first." He felt for her hands in the darkness. "It's your choice when and how to tell Zander that I'm his father. It's your choice where you live and how you raise him. I get that I made a lot of mistakes and it might take some time to trust me again. You need to get to know me all over again, and I know that you and I have pretty much ruined any chance of being together like we used to be. But I need you to know that I will always love our son. I will support you both financially, emotionally and practically in any and every way you need me to. I will always have his back and your back as his mother. No matter what it takes."

She didn't answer for a minute. Instead they stood there in silence and let the rain beat around them. He wrapped his arms around her and pulled her into his chest. She let her head fall against him.

"I'm sorry," she whispered.

"Me, too," he said.

She slid her arms up around his neck and they held each other in the darkness. His lips met hers and he kissed her for one fleeting moment, until he felt the urge welling up inside him to ask her for more. He found himself wanting to hold her tightly in his arms and promise to never let her go. He wanted to ask her to try again, to wipe away the past, to restart the relationship he'd once taken for granted and tossed away.

But instead the knowledge of everything he'd done, everything she'd done, and how much they'd hurt each other seemed to rise up between his heart and his mind like a wall he didn't know how to break. He let go of her and stepped away.

Rain pattered on the roof of the abandoned train station. A fire crackled softly in the front entranceway, just under the shelter of the wood-and-metal awning. Tommy sat by the fire, gun at his side, looking out into the night. Erica lay on her back and dozed softly, letting relief and fatigue fill her limbs. They hadn't been able to get the satellite phone to work again and it might be a while before Nick's brothers were able to reach them. But no one had followed them on the trek from the river to the abandoned railway station. The train had derailed on the other side, putting an entire river between them and the people who'd wanted to hurt them.

She thought of the laptop disappearing into the river, of Clark's and Julie's deaths, of the crew who'd been stranded at the side of the tracks in the rain and of the passengers who'd witnessed weapons being drawn and felt their lives being threatened. There was still so much she didn't know. Like who'd hired Mr. Grand in the first place and how'd they had known about the whistle-blower and the laptop transfer. Who had thought the contents of the laptop was worth hijacking a train and killing a rising-star politician over? And why couldn't Julie hack the data? Was there really nothing there? How had Nick missed a gun when they were searching the criminals and which one of them had somehow got through the door and shot Julie? Where had Bob gone when he'd got off the train?

There was still so much she didn't know. But some things that thankfully she did. Rescue would arrive, the storm would break and the sun would rise. They'd be safe. They'd be found. Now all they could do was wait.

She looked over to the other side of the room where Nick lay asleep on his back with Zander curled up in the crook of his arm. She'd fallen asleep holding her son, while Nick and Tommy were still building the fire. She wasn't even sure when Zander had crawled away from her and over to Nick. But now, there he was, curled up asleep against him.

His father.

Yes, that was something else she knew with absolute certainty. Despite how many times she'd told herself, in the face of Clark's unwanted advances, that Zander didn't need a father, now that she saw her little boy curled up against Nick she knew without the shadow of a doubt in her heart that Zander needed Nick, and Nick seemed to need Zander just as much in return.

Lord, I'm so thankful that You brought Nick into our lives. Thank You that he was there on that train today. Thank You that he rescued Zander. But I don't know where we go from here. I don't know how this is going to impact our lives or how I tell Zander the truth about his father? How do I trust Nick and let him back into my life knowing he might run again? Knowing he might let me down again?

Suddenly she couldn't let herself lie still any longer. This moment of peace and quiet wouldn't last. Rescue would be arriving soon, then she and Zander would go home and Nick would return to base. She had to figure out her heart and mind by then. She had to figure out where she wanted things to go from here. She pushed herself to her feet and started to pace. The small abandoned station had a ticket booth in the front, two customer lounges on either side and a railway shed at the back. She turned toward the shed.

"You okay?" Tommy whispered.

She nodded but somehow her lips wouldn't form the word *yes*. She waved to her brother, crossed through the second customer lounge and then down a long hallway to the train shed. The shed was empty. The smell of wet wood filled her senses. Her footsteps clacked on the worn wooden floor. She walked over to the wide railway doors and looked out across the wild and tree-filled landscape.

I loved him, Lord. I loved Nick with my whole heart. At one point I thought I would've given anything to build a life, a family and a future with him. But I can't just ignore and forget everything that happened. I can't pretend he didn't make the mistakes he did. I can't pretend I didn't make the mistakes I made or the choices I made, either. How will we ever look at each other without seeing all that? How do we ever get past it and try again?

She stood there staring out at the rain. The

storm was lightening. The clouds were turning gray and gold on the horizon. The floorboards creaked behind her.

"Hey, sis?"

She turned. Tommy was standing there behind her in the train shed. One pant leg was soaked dark red from where the bullet had grazed his leg. She'd had to practically drag him across the submerged railway bridge, clinging to the rails and battling the water until they'd finally reached the shore. Only then had she been able to check his wound, help him bandage it up as best they could with the first-aid kit Nick had left her and then break off a branch strong enough to use as a crutch. Even then—with first her, and then her and Nick helping to support Tommy's weight—it had been a long slow trek up the bank and eventually to the abandoned station.

"You shouldn't be standing," she said. "You've lost a lot of blood."

Her brother nodded like he hadn't heard her. He reached into his jacket pocket. "This isn't exactly easy, but I've got to tell you I'm sorry..."

"Stop it!" She raised her hand. "Nobody blames you for what happened. You were shot.

You didn't mean to drop Zander. He knows it. I know it. Everyone knows it. You're the one who stuck that life vest on him. If it weren't for you, he'd have drowned. And don't even start on the fact you accepted Clark's invitation to join him in the first-class cabin. Yes, you knew he had something up his sleeve, but you had no idea how any of this was going to go down."

"I'm sorry I didn't tell you the truth about Nick coming to see you!" Tommy's voice rose. "Stop thinking you know what everyone's thinking, sis, and let me talk!

"I'm sorry that I thought I knew better than you! I'm sorry that when you were pregnant, and Nick came to talk to you, I lied to him and then lied to you about our conversation. I'm not sorry I didn't tell him about Zander, because it wasn't my place to tell him that he was a father. I'm not sorry for trying to protect you and I still don't think he was good enough for you. But I'm sorry I didn't tell you that he came to see you and that I didn't give you the choice. Okay? Because I was wrong. You're plenty strong and smart enough to decide who you want to love. Even if I don't like them."

She blinked. His voice had risen but it was more like he was yelling at himself that her.

"Also, I'm sorry I never gave you this," he said. That was when she realized he was holding his wallet in his hand. He opened his wallet, reached into a plastic side compartment and pulled out a folded piece of paper from behind his driver's license and insurance.

"Nick had this letter for you. I didn't know what to do with it when he gave it to me. I wasn't going to give it to you because he had no right to ask anything of you. It didn't seem right to throw it out, because you were pregnant with his kid and all, and it seemed like the kind of thing you might want to have one day. But I wasn't gonna just stick it somewhere where it might get lost. So I shoved it in my wallet. It got kinda damp, mostly at the edges. But hopefully you can still read it, or some of it anyway."

He dropped the folded piece of paper into her hand. She looked down. It was white ruled paper that looked like it had been torn from a notebook. The text was written in blue ink, double-sided and smudged at the edges.

"Just read it, okay?" Tommy said. He ran his hand over his head. "I don't know what it says. But it belongs to you and I shouldn't have stopped you from reading it. I'll leave you to it. I gotta go think or pray or something." He paused for a moment, like he was trying to decide whether a hug was in order. She didn't give him the choice. She slipped her arms around her brother and hugged him. He patted her on the back. "Be smarter than me, okay? Make better choices. Here, you might need this, too." He handed her a flashlight. Then he turned and walked away.

She waited until he left the shed, then unfolded the paper slowly. She spread it out on the window ledge. It fell apart immediately into four equal squares and it took her a moment to piece it back together. She ran the light over it and read, filling in the gaps as best she could.

The date was seven months before Zander was born.

Erica,
I don't know what to write or how to start this. You've always been better at words. I'm not asking you for anything. There's just some stuff I gotta tell you.

One. I like you. A lot. I've always liked you a lot. I should've told you that more. I should've shouted from the rooftop, "Erica Knight is my girlfriend!"

Two. I'm never going to drink again.

Ever. You probably heard I crashed Max's car and got tossed in the drunk tank. I wish that wasn't true but it totally is. I was stupid. Really, really stupid. Nothing like spending all night in a room I couldn't leave to make me figure out what I care about and what I want.

You know what the hardest thing about it was? What I hated most? That I couldn't talk to you. That I couldn't tell you that being your boyfriend was the most important thing I'd ever done. That you're the most important thing to me.

So I prayed instead. I prayed a lot. I told God I was sorry and that I'd straighten my life out and I'd stop using what happened to my sister as an excuse.

Three. I joined the military. I started basic training last week. I might be hard to reach for a while. But if you give a letter to my parents or my brothers, they'll get it to me.

Four. Look, I know I didn't do or say the things I should've. I know it'll take a long, long time to rebuild your trust. But I'm willing to do it. If you'll have me back. If you'll let me. I'll just show you every day,

day after day, that I'm changing. We'll go to church together. You'll come over and have dinner with my family. I'll hold your hand in public. I'll buy you flowers. I'll learn to play guitar and sing to you. Whatever it takes. Until you get to see and trust that I really mean it and I'm never running away again.

Because I really, really—

The words bled away in a blur of blue ink. Tears rushed to her eyes. She pressed her hands into her eyes and stepped out into the petering rain. She walked, pushing her body through the trees and letting the soft, gentle patter beat her head. The ground sloped steeply upward. She glanced back now and then at the station below, keeping it always in her sight as she climbed. She didn't know how long she'd walk or how far she'd get. Just that after everything that had happened she needed silence and time alone before she went back and joined the men. She swung the flashlight back and forth over the ground and watched the faint, gentle, lightening gray of the day breaking somewhere at the horizon.

Soon enough, Nick and Zander would be

awake, and rescue would arrive. She needed to know her heart and mind by then. And maybe she already did.

Lord, I want this. I want to be with Nick. I want to love him and for him to love me. I want us to be a family. I've always loved him. I've just been so scared that he wouldn't love me back, that he'd run away and that he'd let me down. Help me trust him. Help me love him. Somehow bridge the gap between our hearts.

Footsteps crackled in the woods behind her. She wasn't alone. Hope rose in her chest, thinking Nick had woken and followed her. But just as quickly as it rose, it crashed back down as she turned and looked in horror at the man in a waterproof engineer's jacket and hat standing behind her.

"Bob?" she breathed.

He stepped closer. She swung the light up to his face. No. No, it wasn't. The flashlight fell from her hand and rolled down the hill behind her.

"Clark?" she gasped. Mud and blood streaked his body. A gun was clutched in his hands. "How are you here? Mr. Grand shot you in the head. I watched him throw your body off the train."

"Hey, Erica." A tight smile turned Clark's

lips, as smooth and slimy as it had always been, and coming nowhere near his cold and life-less eyes. "Yeah, you did, didn't you? Only that wasn't me. That was the engineer. Bob something? Mr. Grand pretended to shoot me. Then he forced Bob to switch clothes with me, promising he'd let him go if he did, and then shot him in the head. You watched him throw Bob off the train, thinking it was me. And you didn't even shed a tear. Even now you don't look happy to see me." He shook his head, dis-gust curled at the corner of his smile. "I really went to bat for you, and you let me down."

"I let you down," Erica repeated. Did he hear himself? Standing there in a dead man's clothes and yet acting like he was somehow the vic-tim. Her voice rose. "How did I let you down?"

"I had a plan!" he shouted. "A really good one! Some of my campaign staff apparently didn't like how I treated them and threatened they were going to go to the police and tell them I received secret campaign donations from wealthy Canadian businessmen with ties to organized crime. Me! Like I'm going to be-lieve some of my guys are criminals just be-cause some investigation into a diamond mine in the Arctic, headed by Nick Henry's brother, says so. It was a lie. It had to be a lie! And I couldn't prove it. But I could change the story."

Erica shook her head. He was so determined to believe his wealthy donors were good guys, he wasn't even willing to believe he could've been duped. "So, you decided to become the victim of the train heist linked to the very investigation you wanted to disprove."

"Not the victim. The hero!" Clark shouted. "Mr. Grand was supposed to threaten you, steal the case and tie you up in the storage locker. I was supposed to rescue you. Tommy and Zander were going to see people with guns but never be in actual physical danger. Then the story would get out, and it would be this whole dramatic thing to rehabilitate my career. It didn't matter if there was nothing on the laptop, because eventually I'd be proved right! In the meantime, all everyone would care about was the fact that Ontario's youngest Member of Provincial Parliament tried to meet a whistle-blower, got kidnapped, saved the girl, became a hero."

Of all the emotions sweeping over her—fear, dread, anger, fury—none of them was a surprise. No, this was exactly the kind of stunt he'd pull. He'd always been this man. He always would be.

"But you weren't counting on Nick, were you?" she asked. "That's what ruined everything. That's why everyone was scrambling and you kept coming up with wilder and more dangerous plans, like pretending to be dead and separating the train. See, I'm guessing the criminals only had the basic outline of what to do and honestly believed they were stealing real data. What happened? Couple of the thugs went rogue and tried to actually hijack the train? Mr. Grand tried to double-cross you and make a copy of the data for himself, only Julie couldn't find what wasn't there? Because you didn't let them in on the fact it was nothing but a stunt?"

"It wasn't a stunt!" Clark's voice rose.

"It was totally a stunt," she said. "You hired criminals, you hijacked a train, you risked people's lives for a selfish, reckless, publicity stunt! And don't even pretend you didn't rope my brother into it because you thought you could manipulate him. Or that you wanted to use my son as leverage to manipulate Tommy and me. And what was my role? To fall into your arms?

Because a pretty wife and cute stepson were good for your image?"

"I'm not going to dignify that with an answer!" Clark snapped. "Nobody was supposed to get hurt!"

"You killed two people!" Erica yelled. "I'm guessing you're the one who shot Julie in the back trying to escape. Were you hiding in a sleeper cabin with a gun, orchestrating this whole thing?"

He shrugged. So that was a yes. "I couldn't let her take the laptop."

"Because there were no files. Because there was no hidden data. Because Nick's brother Trent wasn't involved in a faulty investigation. You didn't need actual data. You just needed the hint of it. You disgust me." She shook her head. He raised the gun higher. "Yeah, I see the weapon. But I've been held at gunpoint and shot at more than enough for one night."

"Difference is that none of the people who shot at you were authorized to kill you," he said.

He stepped closer. "The guns weren't even supposed to be real or loaded, not that anybody followed my directions on that. And eventually I realized Fox, Orson and Lou were right to have brought real guns. But you, your brother and your kid were completely off-limits. I tried to spare you. But now, thanks to you, it's too late for that. Now I've gotta be the only one left standing for any of this to work."

Her chin rose, even as she felt tears building in her eyes. "If you're going to shoot me, shoot me now."

"Not until you show me where the others are," Clark said. "Then I'm going to end this once and for all. Don't fight me. Do what I say and I promise it'll all be over quickly. Believe it or not, I care about you, your kid and your brother. I'll make sure Zander won't even see it coming and none of you feel a thing. But I have no choice. I'll make it look like your hothead brother set up the heist to pay off his debts, then he snapped and killed you and Zander before turning the gun on himself when I tried to stop him, leaving me the only survivor."

THIRTEEN

"Wake up, you idiot! And go find Erica!"
Tommy's booming voice jolted Nick awake.
The man's large hand shook his shoulder.

Nick opened his eyes. Pale gray light was filtering through the window. Zander was asleep
by his side, curled up on Nick's army jacket.
Tommy was leaning over him, shaking him like
he was trying to get marbles out of a pop can.
Nick looked around the room. "Where's Erica?"

"I don't know." Tommy stopped shaking him
and crouched down beside him. He was holding a dirty flashlight in his hand. "I had a talk
with her and I finally gave her your letter. You
know the one, the long, rambling one you gave
me to give her like six years ago? Well, I kept
it in my wallet. And I gave it to her, and I told
her I was sorry. Then she went off walking in
the woods and she didn't come back."

Nick eased Zander onto the floor and stood. "What do you mean she didn't come back? How long has she been gone?"

"I don't know. Like ten minutes. I figured I'd give her a moment to read in peace. When I got back she was gone. But the flashlight I gave her was lying partway up the hill, still on." He held it up. "Maybe she just propped the flashlight up somewhere so she wouldn't get lost and could find her way back, and it fell. Maybe she'll come back when she's ready. But I figured either way you're the one who should be going after her. Because I'm injured and you're her guy."

Her guy. Something swelled inside him. He let out a long breath. "Which way did she go?"

"Out the back door of the train shed and then straight up the hill. That's all I know."

Nick paused. He readied himself and then reached for his gun.

"Here, take it." He held it out to Tommy. "If anything happens, use it to defend Zander."

Tommy nodded seriously. He took the weapon. "I will," he said. "I won't let anything happen to your kid, Nick. I know I'm not always a good guy. And that you and I have had our differences. But I love that kid and I'll protect him with my life. I promise."

Nick met his eyes and nodded. "I know." Then he clasped him on the shoulder. "I'm sorry, too. We're good."

Now he just had to pray that Erica was okay. He turned and strode through the train station. It had been almost six years since he'd written that letter, and while he couldn't remember many of the words, the way he'd felt when he'd written it was still engraved on his heart. The storage shed was empty. He crossed through it, went out the doors and up the hill, following the telltale signs of scuffed earth and bent twigs that told him someone had passed that way. He climbed the hill, fighting the urge to shout her name in case she wanted time alone.

Lord, I don't know what she's going to think when she reads that letter. Or where my future is headed. I just know that everything in my heart is calling me toward Erica and our son. You have guided me so well these past years and I'm so grateful for everything I am now and everything that's become of my life. Whatever happens next, please guide and help me make Erica and Zander a part of it.

Broken branches lay ahead of him. Then he

saw two sets of footprints and the signs of a struggle. Two people had fought here. One had been dragged. His heart pounded like a war drum.

Help me, Lord! What happened? Where's Erica? Please let her be okay!

"Erica!" He ran, shouting her name, following the scuffed footprints and broken branches and the story they told. Someone had startled her. He'd grabbed her and dragged her. She'd fought him off and run in the opposite direction of the train shed, leading her attacker away from her son. He'd tackled her. She'd hit the ground. But still, she hadn't given up the fight.

And then the trees broke. He hit a wide cement platform and the remains of what he guessed had once been a storage yard. And lost the trail.

Help me, Lord! Where did they go? Help me find her. He sprinted across the cement and pressed forward. He strained his ears and heard nothing but the wind brushing the trees as the early morning broke from behind the clouds. *I don't even know where I'm going!*

"Erica! Can you hear me?"

"Nick!" Her voice was faint in the distance, but oh, how he'd take it. He ran toward it, press-

ing his body through the woods. Then the trees
parted. A steep rocky incline lay in front of
him. He looked down. A man in a train engineer's rain jacket had Erica by the waist and
was trying to drag her backward while she
kicked and flailed against him.

Desperately, Nick scanned the rocks ahead of
him. How did they get down there? How was
he going to get down there?

For a second he stood, helpless in his indeci-
sion, and watched as Erica swung her elbows
back, catching the man in the jaw. He let go and
she fell free. And Nick suddenly realized who
it was. *Clark?* He didn't know how. He didn't
want to know. All that mattered was that Erica
was now running away from him and that Nick
had to find a way, a path, something, to get
down there and help her.

Clark leaped after her, grabbed her by the
hair and yanked her to him. With a warrior
scream, she spun back and struck him in the
face. Anger pulsed through Nick's core as he
watched the man swing again, his hand making contact and Erica's jaw snapping back. He
wondered if this was how Erica had felt every
time she'd watched him get into a fight. She fell
to the ground, rolled, then sprang back, hands

raised to defend herself. Fierce protective pride beat through Nick's heart. Erica was strong, she was powerful and she was fighting back. He was going to make sure she never had to face another battle alone.

He took a breath, then launched himself over the edge of the rock side, bracing himself with one hand as he climbed down, leaping from ledge to ledge as quickly as he dared.

"Nick!" Erica cried. "Clark has a gun!"

But it was too late. The weapon swung in Clark's hand. He aimed at Nick.

Nick realized he was out in the open on the cliff side with nowhere to run, nowhere to hide and no way to dodge a bullet. *Lord, this is not how I wanted to go, but if this is it, please take care of those I love.*

He heard Clark fire and the sound of the bullet hitting the rock face beside him. He looked down. Erica had thrown herself at Clark. He couldn't see what had happened to the weapon.

Nick's heart stuttered. Erica had saved his life.

He would never let her down again. He gritted his teeth, gave up on the climbing, tucked his chin and let himself fall. He curled into a ball and shielded his head. He tumbled down the rock, a hundred blows smacking against his body.

Lord, Erica accused me once of not being willing to take a hit for her. And while this isn't what she meant, I'd take every single one of these blows and a thousand more to keep her safe.

He hit the ground and, for a second, he couldn't move. Pain radiated through his body and pounded through his brain. The sound of Erica fighting for her life floated somewhere on the edge of his consciousness. No, he was not going to pass out. He was not going to leave her. Not now, not ever.

"Nick!"

"Coming!" He forced the word through his lips, rolled over onto his hands and knees and forced his eyes to open.

Erica was on the ground, pinned by Clark on top of her. The man's hands chained her throat, choking the breath from her lungs. A faint cry left her lips.

Nick dragged himself to his feet and charged at Clark, pulling him off her and tackling him to the ground. They hit the dirt in a battle of limbs. Clark's blows flew at him again and again. And, for a moment, it took all the strength in Nick's depleted body to block the blows.

"You messed everything up!" Clark shouted, his words pounding with splintering pain into Nick's throbbing skull. "You're a nothing, Nick Henry. You get that? You were born a nobody and you'll die a nobody. You'll never be smart. You'll never be powerful. You'll never be rich."

Yeah, maybe not. But with God's grace he might be loved.

Nick ducked the blow, waited until Clark's fist hit the ground and then flung the man off him into the dirt. This time Nick wasn't running away. This time he wasn't letting go. Nick latched his arms around Clark's neck from behind and tightened his grip in a choke hold. And Nick wasn't going to waste his time fighting or trying to prove he was the man. All that mattered right now was ending this quickly and safely, and then throwing his arms around the beautiful woman who was now looking up at him with a gaze he wished he could bottle and keep with him every day of his life. For a moment he thought Clark was going to fight the choke. And then felt Clark's hand smack his arm as the man tapped out.

"Good choice." Nick eased his arm from the

man's throat and let him gasp a breath. Then he flipped him over and pressed his face in the dirt. Nick tore two strips from his own jacket with the help of his pocketknife and used them to tie Clark's hands and legs so he wouldn't run. Then he tore off another and used it to gag Clark's mouth. He was sure Clark had plenty to say. But right now he wanted to talk to Erica uninterrupted.

Nick stood slowly and turned to Erica. She walked toward him and he toward her, until they met, toe-to-toe, several feet from where Clark lay bound and fuming. The clouds broke, and the morning sun rose behind her. Her body was soaked and streaked with mud. Her hair flew wild and loose around her. Her limbs were scratched and bloody.

"You literally look like you've just been dragged backward through the woods," he said. She laughed. "And I've never seen anyone look more beautiful in my life."

He spread his arms and she flew into him. She clutched him and he held her against his chest, like she was the missing piece of him and they never wanted to let each other go.

"It was a setup," Erica gasped. "Clark confessed. The whole time it was a fraud. He hired

Mr. Grand and his thugs, who double-crossed him and went rogue—"

"I'm in love with you." Nick took her face in his hands as he blurted out the words that had crossed his mind countless times but that he'd never had the courage to say. "Erica Knight. I am so very deeply and truly in love with you. I feel like I've loved you my entire life and I should've told you that a million times before. But I love you. I always have loved you and I always will."

"I love you, too, Nick." Tears filled the beautiful depths of her eyes. "You have no idea how much I love you. Why did you fall down the cliff instead of taking the path?"

"I couldn't find the path."

She laughed. Then she held him, and she kissed him. And they stood there with their arms around each other for what felt like both an eternity and a moment wrapped in one. She didn't even look up when they heard the sound of rescue helicopters circling above them or two male voices that could only be Nick's brothers teasingly calling out to him or Clark being taken away or even Tommy's voice in the distance. No, she held on to him and kissed his face and he kissed her tears, in front of a crowd of rescue people gathering around them, until the moment they heard one voice cut through them all.

"Mommy! Why are you kissing Soldier Nick?"

She pulled away and he let her go. She wiped her hands over her eyes, then knelt and opened her arms for her son—their son—as his father dropped to the ground beside him.

"Because Nick is your daddy, Little Soldier," she said, the words choking with tears in her throat and sending love surging through her core. "We lost each other for a while. But you went and found him. Your uncle Tommy was wrong in what he said about your daddy. Your daddy is actually very good and very brave, just like you."

Zander's green eyes looked up at Nick, wide and full of hope. "For real? You're my for-real daddy?"

"For real and forever," Nick said. He glanced at Erica. "I promise."

Then she scooped Zander up and Nick wrapped his arms around them both, holding the woman and boy.

The early-June sun was beginning its descent over the Ontario sky as Erica pulled her pickup down the old, familiar road to the Henry family farm. The warm and welcoming farmhouse with its large wooden porch hadn't changed all that much since she'd run through the woods over here as a teenager. Neither had the way her heart skipped a beat as her eyes fell on the tall, broad-shouldered form of the man standing at the edge of the driveway.

Nick Henry. The man she loved. The man who loved her. The father of her child.

"Hey, Daddy!" Zander yelled, leaning out the open window and waving enthusiastically with both hands. "We brought cupcakes! I helped with the sprinkles! They're blue!"

Nick laughed, "That sounds awesome."

She barely managed to park and help Zander out of his booster seat before he launched out of the truck and into his father's arms. She parked the car, grabbed the cooler bag with the cupcakes from the back seat and climbed out as Nick swung Zander around.

Then man and boy stopped spinning and Nick turned to her. His gaze fell on her face and the depths of love in his eyes sent heat rising to her cheeks. A teasing grin crossed his mouth. "How's my girlfriend?"

"Daddy, that's silly," Zander said. He slithered from Nick's arms and onto the ground. "Mommy is way too old to be a *girl* friend."

Light twinkled in Nick's eyes. "Oh, believe me, I know."

So did she. In the six weeks since their lives had been thrown together during the train hijacking, she'd got the impression more than once that Nick had been on the verge of asking her to marry him, but each time he changed the subject at the last moment, leaving her wondering. Maybe he was waiting for the right place and time. Maybe he was waiting to make it perfect. Maybe he was waiting to find the right words. Or waiting for some indication from her that she was ready and that she thought the timing was right.

Well, she was and she did. Back when she was a teenager she'd spent way too many days and nights waiting for Nick Henry to ask her to be his girlfriend instead of stepping up and asking him. A smile curved her lips as she slid the cooler bag over her shoulder and started toward the house. She was done waiting. A black tungsten ring engraved with three silver maple leaves sat snugly in her front pocket. It was simple, masculine, patriotic, and it suited him perfectly. And when the time was right, she was going to ask the man she loved to marry her.

They walked toward the house, Zander in between, holding each other's hands. "Grandma and Grandpa Henry are going to be here for dinner, right?"

"Right." Nick smiled. "Also Uncle Jacob, Uncle Trent, Auntie Chloe, Uncle Max and Auntie Daisy."

"Is Baby Fitz here, too?" Zander beamed.

"Absolutely, Fitz is here," Nick said. He chuckled. Out of all his new relatives, Zander seemed to like his new toddler cousin most of all.

Zander pulled away from Nick's grasp and ran for the door, then stopped, doubled back and stuck his arms out. "Can I carry the bag? I wanna show Fitz the cupcakes."

"Okay," Erica said. "Just be very, very careful. Okay?"

He nodded earnestly. She eased the bag off her shoulder and into his hands. Zander grabbed the cooler with both hands and ran for the farmhouse. She watched as he leaped up the stairs, the front door opened and Jacob let him in. He waved at Erica and Nick, then closed the door. She reached for Nick's hand

and their pace slowed as he linked his fingers through hers.

"I can't believe how wonderful your family is with him," she said. "I hope the cupcakes are still in one piece when they get to the table. But if they're not, I know your family will somehow make it okay."

"They will." Nick's fingers ran slowly over hers. "They love him so much. How did things go with therapy?"

Erica had taken a three-month leave from work after the hijacking and had been taking Zander to Toronto once a week to meet with a child and family psychologist about what had happened.

"Good," she said. "Theresa Dean is really great with him. She says we can't know what the long-term impact of a childhood trauma like that is going to be and that what he experienced will shape him forever. But that children are very resilient and we can surround him with the love and resources he needs to get through."

Nick nodded. "Yeah, I get that."

"I know you do."

Thankfully, it seemed the various members of the heist crew were all turning on each other in a hurry to cut a deal and testify against each other. Tommy had agreed to step up and work with prosecutors to give full testimony at the trial, which should spare both her and Zander the stand.

Thank You, God, that no matter what comes, my son is sharing his life with a father and family that will be there for him.

Not that she was expecting the entire Henry clan to be at the farmhouse when she asked Nick to marry her. But on the other hand, maybe it's the way Nick would've wanted it. "Can we walk for a bit before we head in? I'd like some time to talk to you alone."

He blinked. "Everything okay?"

She tightened her grip on his hand. "Very much so."

There was the sound of a car coming up the gravel driveway behind them. She turned. It was a shiny, nondescript black sedan. "Expecting anyone else?"

"No." Nick's forehead wrinkled. The car stopped, a man got out wearing blue jeans, a black shirt and sunglasses. He somehow had the look of a man who was incredibly reliable and yet utterly forgettable. Nick blinked. "Oh, wow."

"What?" Erica asked. The man was vaguely

familiar, but she wasn't sure where she'd seen him before. "Was he on the train?"

"That's Liam Bearsmith. The man who secured the back half of the train and called for help. I have no idea what he's doing here. I haven't seen him since that night." He tugged her forward. "Come on, you've got to meet him."

Nick dropped her hand and strode across the driveway toward him, arm outstretched. "Well, if it isn't Liam Bearsmith, the purported real estate agent."

There was a slight glimmer of a grin on Liam's face but a full-on smile in his eyes.

"Liam will do." He shook Nick's hand firmly. "And you still owe me a motorcycle." Then he turned to Erica and reached for her hand. "It's wonderful to meet you. I'm very glad to hear that you and your son are well."

"Thank you." Erica returned the handshake. "I'm glad to meet you, too. I'll resist the urge to ask what you really do for a living, but I gather it's important."

The man nodded. A distant look crossed his eyes. "I find things of immense value that were lost, sometimes a very long time ago, and do my best to return them to where they belong. I'm sorry to interrupt a family meal, but I needed to talk to Trent, Jacob and Chloe, and I understand they're all here."

"By all means." Nick gestured to the house. "This won't be the first family meal interrupted by their work. Don't be surprised if my mom tries to talk you into staying for dinner."

Liam nodded and as he turned and headed for the house Erica could sense a question burning in Nick's mind. One she knew Nick shouldn't and couldn't ask.

"Liam?" she called. The man stopped. "I know you can't answer the question, but I need to ask it anyway. Have you found the man who killed Faith?"

Sadness washed over Liam's features and for a moment she wondered who he'd once lost. "Not yet," he said. "But I firmly believe everything lost is found eventually. No matter how long it takes. I have to."

He walked toward the house. Nick and Erica watched him go. She brushed her hand along Nick's arm. Yes, she had to believe that nothing and no one was ever lost forever. She and Nick had lost each other for far too long but had finally found each other again. She would never lose him again.

Nick pulled his arm away and ran his hand across the back of his neck. "I had something planned for later, but maybe tonight's not the night."

She turned to face him. "Well, I had something planned, too, and even though the timing is terrible, I love you, Nick Henry, and I don't want to wait a second longer."

She reached into her pocket and felt the smoothness of the tungsten ring against her fingers. *Help me, Lord. This is the scariest thing I've ever done but also the most right.* She pulled out the ring, debated getting down on one knee and decided to stay standing.

"Nick, I've loved you for as long as I can remember. You're an amazing father to our son and the best friend I've ever had—"

"Stop!" Nick's hand shot out and clamped over her lips. His eyes darted, panicked, to the ring in her outstretched fingers. "Don't do what I think you're about to do!"

Was he really stopping her from proposing? She pushed his hand off and stepped back. "No, Nick, let me say this. I know you've never been good at romantic stuff, or saying the right words, and maybe that's okay. Maybe I can be the one to say the words this time."

His eyes looked to the house, up to the sky and then back to her face. "Wait, don't—"

"No, Nick, I need to say this. Please listen. For me, even if you don't say yes—"

"You're impossible and I love you." An exasperated laugh left his handsome mouth. Then to her surprise he reached down, wrapped his arms around her waist and lifted her into his arms. He took off running across the field, toward the barn, holding her to his chest. "Just give me two seconds, okay, and then you can say whatever you want to say?"

"What are you doing?" Was he really going to carry her across the farm without telling her why? "You're going to make me drop the ring!"

"Just hold on to it! One second! We're almost there!"

He crossed the field, rounded the barn and stopped. There lay the woods stretching between her farm and his, and the same path they'd each run to many times to see each other. He put her down on a bench.

She looked around. "This is new. When did you put a bench here?"

Nick laughed and panted, "Yesterday!"

Then the full sight of what she was seeing hit

her eyes. Fairy lights had been wrapped around the trees. Lights hung from the branches.

He followed her gaze. "There's no point turning them on until the sun sets. But it's really pretty. I bought every string of white Christmas lights the guy at the hardware store could dig out."

Her hand rose to her lips. "You were…"

"Going to propose tonight?" he finished. "Yeah, after dinner with my family. Everybody's in on it. After dinner we were going to go for a walk and then I was going to bring you here, while my family set up for a surprise engagement party. I invited your brother, Tommy, and some of our friends from high school. I wanted everybody to know that I was yours and you were mine."

A smile crossed her lips. "You sound really confident I was going to say yes."

A grin turned up one corner of his mouth. He looked down at the ring in her hands. "Maybe I was. Or maybe I was just really hopeful." He reached into his back pocket and pulled out a sheet of ruled paper. Words spilled down both sides. "I also wrote a really great proposal. Got my brothers and parents to help me practice it and everything. But maybe we don't need it."

The man she loved knelt down on one knee. Then he hesitated.

"Do you want to go first?" Nick asked. "Because I really don't want to steal your moment."

She laughed. Her hand rose to her lips. "No, no, go ahead."

Something in her heart needed to hear him say the words.

"Okay." He fished a ring box out of his pocket and opened it. A beautiful platinum ring sat inside, a large diamond in the middle and a small green emerald on either side.

"Erica Knight, I'm in love with you," Nick said. "You're beautiful, gutsy and strong. You challenge me. You're an amazing mother to our son. You love me better than I deserve. You're a perfect fit for me. Babe, will you marry me?"

"Of course! Will you marry me?"

"Absolutely." He chuckled. "Indefinitely and forever."

Then she leaned forward and kissed his lips, deeply and lovingly, while he slid his ring onto her finger and she slid her ring onto his.

* * * * *

*If you enjoyed this story,
look for the other books
in the True North Heroes series:*

Undercover Holiday Fiancée
The Littlest Target

Dear Reader,

As I write this I am down to my last few days of finishing this book. I took a break from writing today to go visit the small rural train station where I first got the idea for this story. It was fun to walk around the train and to picture how my hero would look clinging to the outside.

Last summer I volunteered to be a train attendant for a mystery event set on a train as it rolled through the Ontario countryside. The conductor was a real character and had a lot of interesting conspiracy theories he thought would make good books. Instead, I asked for his suggestions on how to hijack the train. And while a lot of this book is very much fiction, including the liberties I took with train layout, operations and route, I definitely have to thank him for giving me the idea.

I really enjoyed coming back to writing about the Henry brothers. Nick and Erica's love story really touched my heart and I hope you enjoyed it, too!

Thank you so much to everyone who has written to me about the Henry brothers, especially those who wanted to know why Trent and Chloe's engagement has lasted over a year, if the cold case of Faith's murder will ever be solved and if her killer will face justice. I'm starting on my final book about the Henry brothers soon and can't wait to share the final chapter of the family's story with you. In the meantime, keep your thoughts and questions coming!

You can find me on Twitter at @MaggieKBlack, on Facebook and at www.maggiekblack.com.

Thank you all for sharing this journey with me.

Maggie

Get 4 FREE REWARDS!

We'll send you 2 FREE Books plus 2 FREE Mystery Gifts.

Love Inspired® books feature contemporary inspirational romances with Christian characters facing the challenges of life and love.

FREE
Value Over
$20

Get 4 FREE REW

We'll send y

plus 2 FREE M

TH

**Harlequin® Heartwarm
Larger-Print** books
feature traditional
values of home, family,
community and—most of
all—love.

FREE
Value Over
$20

YES! Please send me 2 FREE Harlequin® Heartwarming™ Larger-Print novels and my
2 FREE mystery gifts (gifts worth about $10 retail). After receiving them, if I don't wish
to receive any more books, I can return the shipping statement marked "cancel." If I
don't cancel, I will receive 4 brand-new larger-print novels every month and be billed
just $5.49 per book in the U.S. or $6.24 per book in Canada. That's a savings of at
least 19% off the cover price. It's quite a bargain! Shipping and handling is just 50¢ per
book in the U.S. and 75¢ per book in Canada.* I understand that accepting the 2 free
books and gifts places me under no obligation to buy anything. I can always return a
shipment and cancel at any time. The free books and gifts are mine to keep no matter
what I decide.

161/361 IDN GMY3

Name (please print)

Address   Apt. #

City   State/Province   Zip/Postal Code

Mail to the **Reader Service:**
IN U.S.A.: P.O. Box 1341, Buffalo, NY 14240-8531
IN CANADA: P.O. Box 603, Fort Erie, Ontario L2A 5X3

Want to try 2 free books from another series! Call 1-800-873-8635 or visit www.ReaderService.com.

---

*Terms and prices subject to change without notice. Prices do not include sales taxes, which will be charged (if applicable)
based on your state or country of residence. Canadian residents will be charged applicable taxes. Offer not valid in Quebec.
This offer is limited to one order per household. Books received may not be as shown. Not valid for current subscribers
to Harlequin Heartwarming Larger-Print books. All orders subject to approval. Credit or debit balances in a customer's
account(s) may be offset by any other outstanding balance owed by or to the customer. Please allow 4 to 6 weeks for delivery.
Offer available while quantities last.

Your Privacy—The Reader Service is committed to protecting your privacy. Our Privacy Policy is available online at
www.ReaderService.com or upon request from the Reader Service. We make a portion of our mailing list available to reputable
third parties that offer products we believe may interest you. If you prefer that we not exchange your name with third parties, or
if you wish to clarify or modify your communication preferences, please visit us at www.ReaderService.com/consumerschoice
or write to us at Reader Service Preference Service, P.O. Box 9062, Buffalo, NY 14240-9062. Include your complete name and
address.

HW19R